# The Helper

# Mary McLaurin

# The Helper

Olympia Publishers
*London*

**www.olympiapublishers.com**
OLYMPIA PAPERBACK EDITION

A CIP catalogue record for this title is
available from the British Library.

ISBN: 978-1-78830-964-6

First Published in 2021

Olympia Publishers
Tallis House
2 Tallis Street
London
EC4Y 0AB

Printed in Great Britain

## Dedication

For my two sons with much love.

# PROLOGUE

It is 8.15 pm on Sunday 5 April 2020 and Her Majesty Queen Elizabeth II has just given her stirring address of hope to the UK and the Commonwealth assuring us that the UK "will succeed" in its fight against the coronavirus pandemic but acknowledging that there may be "more to endure before normality can return to the country". The Queen, looking amazing for nearly ninety-four and regally immaculate in a beautiful dress of a particular shade of turquoise (not unlike the colour of some of the NHS scrubs), thanked frontline NHS staff, care workers and others for "selflessly" carrying out their essential roles during the crisis. She also praised everyday citizens for adhering to the terms of the lockdown and staying at home thus helping to prevent the spread of the virus.

I am sitting on the sofa, in my comfortable home, and I have been very moved by this short message, no more than four minutes, of calm encouragement, belief and thanks. It was so inclusive. The brave NHS staff, the ambulance and fire crews, all working tirelessly to save lives; the nursing home carers who show almost superhuman dedication to their vulnerable charges; the police who uphold the lockdown rules and deal with those who are finding it difficult to surrender their freedom and abide by those rules; and us whose task is simply to stay at home and not go out at all — everyone was mentioned.

I am surviving the lockdown without too many physical

problems but I am definitely suffering from severe frustration at not being able to volunteer and help in this unprecedented crisis. Reading about the community work that has been taken on by so many only serves to highlight my enforced inactivity and lack of ability to be able to help, other than by financial donations. However much I would like to say, loudly, that age is only a number I can understand that this terrifying virus is likely to be more severe in those now over seventy and the requirement for hospital treatment more probable. To contract Covid-19 would not be helping those it had been my intention to help.

Like for so many people, my days are long and difficult to fill. I keep in touch with the children and the grandchildren via WhatsApp, Zoom and Skype which is wonderful and also produces some splendid humour — so there are laughs every day — but I need more if I am to remain sane and not be a burden either to my family or the NHS. My attempts to volunteer to be at the end of the telephone for those in need haven't met with success and so, in desperation for some mental if not social activity, my mind has turned to the time when I had been a helper, not because of a global pandemic and I had been nobly helping others with their struggles, but because I had needed to cope with my own struggles. Thus I am now filling my days and keeping my sanity by putting those struggles and that help into words.

# CHAPTER ONE

It was a Tuesday early in November 1992. The sun sparkled on the sea and the hills on the far side of the estuary were wreathed in a fine mist, one of those splendid, calm autumn mornings.

I locked the front door of the house, did a quick mental check — immersion off, gas fires off, plants watered, rubbish out — took a deep breath and thought, "this is it, I'm really on my own — Mrs Westwood here I come".

If one was foolish enough, or brave enough, depending on how you look at it, to leave one's husband at the age of 45 with no glittering career to fall back on it can be a daunting world out there. The secretarial course, followed by a few years of fitting in a fairly turgid office job with a hectic London social life in the sixties, does not overly impress prospective bosses in the nineties.

I had taken a long hard look at my array of talents and decided that the only things that I was really any good at were running a house, cooking, gardening, looking after people, adept with the tea and sympathy, experienced at pulling encouragement out of thin air with very little to go on (most mothers who have been through the GCSE and A level traumas with their children are good at that), not so good at cleaning and ironing but do them with a reasonable grace. So what was I equipped to be — a helper? In other words, what I had been doing for the past twenty-three years. The difference being that

now I had to earn a living at it. With the increasing problem of help for the elderly, or those who cannot manage on their own even if this is only a temporary problem, agencies now abound providing such help and I have signed up with one.

When I poured out my plans to my brother, during a hugely expensive transatlantic telephone call, he applauded my initiative but warned me that I would experience at times total exhaustion, at times interminable boredom, houses that were too hot or too cold and people that were boring, fractious or just downright impossible!

I had not been deterred. My husband, Alan, thinks I'm mad (well he thought I was mad to leave him in the first place), my two sons have been wonderfully supportive, but I have a sneaking suspicion they both think that I have just reached a mid-life crisis and most of my friends are quite sure that it won't be long before I come in from the cold.

It was now 8.30 am and I had to be in Warwickshire by mid-day so I couldn't linger, a last glance up at the house and I must be off. I shall miss my house, it is a lovely Victorian terraced house on the seafront of a sleepy Welsh village, one of the good bits about being married into the mafia. I don't mean the genuine Sicilian mafia just, in my mind's eye, Liverpool's answer to it. However, the similarities are the same, a large, selfish, self-centred family (but with some notable exceptions of whom I'm very fond) ruled by wealth, the accumulation and distribution of which being via the family business. The only difference is that this version doesn't carry guns except on the pheasant shoot. Nonetheless they still gobble up the outsiders and fail to spit out the pips, hence my escaping act, but at least their wealth enabled the purchase of this house for holidays and now it had become my

home.

I got into my car with a bag stuffed with my newly acquired mobile phone, jeans, sweaters, vests for the cold, T shirts for the heat, apron, cookery books, and a smart jacket just in case. Wellies and Barbour were thrown into the boot.

Just before leaving I checked in the rear-view mirror to make sure that I had put some lipstick on. Probably Mrs Westwood's eyesight is so bad that she won't even notice but it made me feel better. Unfortunately, the glance was a bad idea because I saw my hair. Yesterday I was so pleased to be actually employed at last that I felt that I must do something about my appearance and that a haircut was required. Consequently, I had burst into the hair salon, full of enthusiasm and asked for a good trim. The hairdresser clearly thought such a request was like manna from heaven, out came her scissors and she was off. Half an hour later I had less a trim and blow dry and more a demolition job. In vain I tried to console myself that the very short bob made me look younger but sadly it didn't, I just look dowdy.

A deep breath, into first gear, another look in the rear-view mirror (this time to check the traffic) and I set off.

The M25 is often described as the largest car park in the world, well, all I can say is that the junction of the M54 and M6 is only marginally smaller. I had decided that the quickest way to Warwickshire would be via the motorways rather than wending my way over the Welsh hills in the mist. I didn't want to have to contend with tractors driving at two miles an hour and flocks of sheep supposedly being moved from one hillside to another but in reality, having a wonderful time blocking the road, thus causing enormous irritation to the sheep dogs and traffic but causing the farmer in charge no concern at all. He

usually just altered his speed from slow to stop!

"What," I asked myself, "is the difference between a road blocked by sheep to a road blocked by cars and lorries?" Either way I was going to be late for my first job with the agency — a fine way to start. Mrs Westwood would be expecting a calm, efficient helper to turn up on her doorstep on time. Instead of which she would have to wait for my arrival in a hassled, anxious and far from competent state.

The Hon Mrs Margaret Westwood is eighty-five years old, a widow and had just come out of hospital after a bout of pneumonia. I had had several conversations with her godson, Mr Kemp, who lives in Bath and he had given me a very comprehensive lowdown on her. Apparently, she is a tremendous character, dictatorial, irascible, likes everything in the right place, very religious and extremely right-wing. Mr Kemp felt that to the right of Attila the Hun described her perfectly. However, what impressed me most was the enormous devotion that she inspired in Mr Kemp. He had undertaken all the arrangements for her because Mrs Westwood has no children of her own or any close family. In fact, her sister had just died. Reading between the lines, if one can do that in a telephone conversation, I suspected that my real raison d'être was to ensure that Mrs Westwood went to her sister's funeral and I'm always prepared to accept a challenge. In the meantime, I had first actually to arrive at her house.

Fortunately, the traffic finally freed itself, an obliging lorry driver allowed me to merge in front of him from the M54 to the M6 and I sped on my way. Actually, the lorry driver probably wasn't obliging in the least. He had just spent 20 minutes watching the various emotions flitting across my face and undoubtedly couldn't bear the thought of suffering the

alternative to allowing me in front of him, in other words total hysterics!

By breaking all speed limits, thank goodness there were no traffic police around, and by luck rather than by good judgement I actually managed to arrive on time. So, even if I was not calm and efficient, I was at least punctual.

Mrs Westwood's home was an attractive house built out of Cotswold stone and situated at the end of a long, weedy and unkempt drive. The impressive oak front door was opened, to my surprise, by a pleasant woman in her 50s. On seeing my rather blank look the lady introduced herself as Alison and explained that she was a neighbour and that she had been helping out until I arrived. It was immediately apparent that Alison has been a tower of strength to Mrs Westwood but who was, quite obviously, thoroughly relieved to see me. Running between two houses had been a lot of work and whilst giving me a cup of coffee, in the large, archaic kitchen, she confided that now I was here she was going to beat a hasty retreat at the weekend and spend a few days with her daughter for a rest. Although further conversation revealed that Alison's daughter was married to a dairy farmer and had two small children so I think a rest was the last thing that she was going to get.

Having finished our coffee Alison said that she would take me into the drawing room to meet Mrs Westwood. In a loud stage whisper she said that Mrs Westwood was feeling very nervous, so again I was taken by surprise — Mr Kemp had certainly made no reference to nervousness with regards to his Godmother, quite the reverse! However, Mrs Westwood looked exactly how I imagined her. A fairly tall lady, who despite her age and slightly bowed shoulders wore her tweed skirt and lambswool sweater with much elegance. Her face,

although very lined, still revealed traces of handsomeness. It was a very strong face and I am sure she had never been strictly beautiful but she had excellent cheekbones and a wide generous mouth. The one thing that I found slightly disconcerting about her was that she never once looked directly at me, but that didn't stop her noticing absolutely everything that went on.

Mrs Westwood greeted me with great charm but I realised later that she really had been nervous. She has a funny little habit of going "humph", and when she gets agitated, she "humphs" all the time, and I could hardly hear her greeting for "humphs"!

Mrs Westwood took me up to the guest room and for 85 she is extremely nimble, she was up the stairs in a flash. The guest room was wonderful. Light poured in through two windows flanked with pretty floral chintz curtains. There were two marvellously comfortable looking beds, an armchair, dressing table, washbasin, a gorgeous antique chest of drawers, an electric fire and a teasmade. Mrs Westwood was very apologetic because she couldn't find the instructions for the teasmade, had I enough towels and please put on the fire whenever I wanted it, apparently the central heating was never used. I felt more like an honoured guest than the helper.

Back downstairs Alison thought it might be helpful if she initiated me into the workings of the Parkray fire in the drawing room. I should have paid more attention to her but I am afraid at the time her instructions went in one ear and straight out of the other.

With a slightly sceptical look Alison left, she knew that I would rue the day I hadn't listened carefully to her pearls of wisdom. Mrs Westwood sat down for a snooze in front of the

Parkray and I was left to explore the house and get my bearings.

Apart from the drawing room there was a small dining room where, according to Alison, Mrs Westwood ate her lunch and dinner using all the silver and best china. The archaic kitchen, which gave onto a larder and then the garage, had clearly never been modernised, except for the Aga which had been converted to oil. The sink was an ancient Belfast sink, enormous and with wonderful old wooden draining boards on either side. The only snag was Mrs Westwood had covered the wood with two dreadful plastic draining boards. Not only did they look horrible but they didn't lie flat and were full of bumps and acted as trampolines when you put anything on them. I dreaded washing up as I spent my entire time rushing to catch the priceless china as it bounced up with every intention of smashing itself to smithereens on the tile floor below. There literally wasn't a cheap piece of china in the house. The cupboards were an Aladdin's cave of Spode, Royal Doulton and Coalport. There wasn't a full set of anything, just a jumble of different pieces but all gorgeous.

The only modern aspect to the kitchen was a brand-new washing machine and a brand-new tumble dryer and these were kept under wraps. Each was covered by a dustsheet around which was tied a decaying piece of string. After I had done the first wash, I neatly folded up the dust sheets and the string and put them on a shelf. Mrs Westwood made no comment but as soon as my back was turned, she put the shrouds back on again. I swiftly learnt my lesson!

That first afternoon I took the tea tray into the drawing room at half past four as requested. I never quite got over the feeling that I ought to bob a curtsey to Mrs Westwood when I

spoke to her (so appropriate when clad in a pair of jeans). Not because she wasn't always the soul of politeness and concern for my well-being, it seemed to slip her mind that I was there to look after her well-being, but because having staff was clearly second nature to her.

I learnt a lot about her family that afternoon. Mrs Westwood had been brought up in Cheshire and the family seemed to have owned quite a few castles dotted around the county. Apparently, her father had succeeded his grandfather to the barony because his own father had pre-deceased him. He had drowned and there had been dark mutterings about foul play, even the doctor had been hesitant about signing the death certificate, but nothing had been proved. Nonetheless Mrs Westwood's forebears had been considerate enough to die in the right order so that instead of two sets of death duties there had only been one. This conjured up a marvellous picture of the Baron and his son politely deciding in which order they must depart this world so as to cheat the government of its pound of flesh!

Mrs Westwood was undoubtedly very right wing and extremely forthright in airing her views. According to her the socialists had definitely killed the goose that lays the golden egg and that this country was never the same after the nation failed to return Winston Churchill at the end of the war. The current young royals were not to be spared either. The Princess of Wales came in for quite a hiding, "the Spencers must have been horrified by her behaviour and should have told her, straight from the shoulder, just how horrified they were, a disgrace to her class!" Sarah Ferguson had rather less of a lambasting, "well after all she had come up from nothing, hadn't she dear, and probably didn't know any better".

I was left feeling slightly stunned. In today's very politically correct world not many people would have given vent to such uninhibited views.

Tea over, with some relief, I next had to tackle dinner. Alison had kindly left a chicken, some potatoes and a cabbage but could I find a tin to roast the chicken in? The only tin I could find was so old and had so many layers of burnt-on grime that it was a health hazard and the dustbin was obviously its appropriate home. Getting slightly desperate, because 7.30 pm was the appointed hour for dinner, I finally unearthed a vast but relatively clean tin. The snag was that it only just fitted into the oven and it certainly didn't slide over the runners. I had to jam it in and heave it out with considerable force which resulted in hot fat spilling all over my feet, clad fortunately, in ancient trainers.

With the main course under way, I turned my thoughts to pudding. The larder was bare except for an ageing bottle of cooking brandy and a miniature of Navy rum. However, the deep freeze revealed some lime ripple ice-cream. Not wanting Mrs Westwood to think that my cooking skills were totally lacking I decided to make a melba sauce out of a half-used, mouldy jar of lime marmalade. The melted marmalade was rather sickly so I tipped in a generous quantity of the brandy to give it a bit of *"je ne sais quoi"*. At this stage total exhaustion was beginning to overcome me — I could just feel my brother sitting on my shoulder saying, "I told you so"! I had brought a bottle of whisky with me so that I could indulge in a drink every evening so I went upstairs to retrieve it. Dinner was going well and I had just finished my very welcome whisky and water when in swept Mrs Westwood, hostess to the last, with an enormous glass of sherry for me. She apologised

for not joining me in a sherry because unfortunately alcohol tended to make her haemorrhage internally and then she swept out of the kitchen again. I briefly debated whether to throw the sherry down the drain as sherry and whisky don't really mix but it seemed such a waste, so I drank it. However, the melba sauce and all that brandy did go down the drain. I didn't want Mrs Westwood's death on my conscience.

After dinner we watched the 9 o'clock news on the television and then Mrs Westwood announced that it was her bedtime but she would just stay to make sure that I did the fire properly. Oh, how I wished that I had listened to Alison more carefully because this fearsome contraption had a will of its own. It sounded quite simple — it had to be riddled, the ash removed and more furnacite banked on so that it would last through the night. With much fumbling and to the background of "my dear it is so simple" I finally managed to lift the cover at the bottom so that I could get at the riddle which had to be pulled energetically 200 times (no more and no less!) Well, I didn't bother to count, which was a mistake, because when I had finished, I apparently had only riddled 172 times. I felt like being back at school doing the correct number of lines for detention. Next, I had to get down on my hands and knees with the poker and clear out the grid from underneath. I did as I was told but obviously not very effectively because all of a sudden, the Hon Mrs Westwood was on her hands and knees, the poker was grabbed out of my hand and with, "this is how you do it gel," down went her head, up went her bottom and she was wielding that poker as if she was on the jousting field. I only slightly retrieved my position in that she couldn't get back up off the floor and had to ask for my assistance. Even putting on the furnacite was not an easy task. I had to dig it out of the hod

with a minute shovel which only held a few pieces. If you filled it too full, when you pulled the shovel out of the hod pieces of furnacite flew off all over the immaculate pale green carpet.

Finally, my tasks were completed and feeling absolutely shattered I retired to bed. The beautiful bedroom seemed calm and welcoming and after a perfunctory wash I slipped between the pristine sheets. As I lay there many thoughts floated through my head — had I done the right thing in leaving my erstwhile comfortable existence for this unknown and, at the moment, rather frightening way of life? I felt alone but then I had been lonely in my marriage, perhaps I should never have married Alan. But then our two sons, Nick and Simon, would never have existed and that was unthinkable. I remembered so well the day that each of them had been born and, although like everyone we have had our moments, they are the lights of my life. I couldn't wish their lives away. Nick was now up at university living life to the full, very independent and home rarely, and Simon was on a gap year prior to university and currently in Egypt policing the coral reef in the Red Sea. Both were now young men with their own lives and careers to forge. Perhaps if we had had a daughter, I would not have felt quite so surplus to requirements.

I had met Alan when he was doing a graduate banking internship with Morgan Stanley in London. Although he had a 2.1 degree in English, he was comfortable with numbers and had a real interest in working in the financial services. Alan was handsome, charming, oh so charming, had a good sense of humour and an enormous circle of friends. I was swept off my feet. For a few enchanted months, life in London was all that I had could possibly have wished it to be. We never

discussed the future, why would we, we were only 23 and 21 years old and having fun.

However, on a weekend spent with Alan's parents he suddenly announced to them that we were getting married. I was dumbfounded. Alan hadn't proposed so where was this coming from. It was too embarrassing to admit the situation in front of his parents so, for the time being I went along with it. The worst thing I could have done. Alan announced that he was not going to go into banking but that he was going to join the family business instead. This meant living not far from this business in the Liverpool area. To me, who had been brought up on a farm in Surrey, loved riding and the countryside, this was akin to living at the ends of the earth. Alan next announced that he had a bought a cottage in the countryside so he was sure I would be happy. I was trapped. I loved Alan and he was so excited about everything. The cottage, when I saw it, was idyllic so I just decided that this was obviously meant to be and got on with wedding plans. It was only later, after we had been married for some time, that I learnt that the head of the mafia had told Alan that if he didn't come into the family business it would be sold. The business was definitely the goose that laid the golden egg and the head of the mafia brought considerable pressure to bear to ensure that Alan joined it. The business needed to exist and thrive in order to support the whole family including Alan's many siblings who certainly didn't want the golden goose to up sticks and die. Alan's announcement to his parents that we were engaged had been to pre-empt any possibility that I might say "No" and it had worked! After this revelation I started to see Alan and the mafia in a very different light, and once that light had been turned on it was very difficult to turn it off.

On and on went the thoughts until I became aware that the bed was neither comfortable nor aired, in fact it was positively damp! I felt icy cold so I put on a sweater over my pyjamas and curled up into a ball and hoped that sleep would come. Eventually, through sheer exhaustion, it did but it was only fitful.

The next morning, I looked pale and as drained as I felt but got dressed quickly because I needed to be downstairs tackling that fiendish Parkray before Mrs Westwood got up. The Parkray had to be dealt with twice a day, it consumed furnacite at an enormous rate and the hods were very heavy and tricky to fill. Definitely not a job for an 85-year-old lady however robust. Why on earth didn't Mrs Westwood dispense with the Parkray and turn on the central heating.

Later on that morning, I was placed in a quandary. My conversations with Mr Kemp made it plain that he felt that his Godmother had now reached the stage when either she needed someone permanently with her or she ought to go into a care home. Even being here less than 24-hours, and despite the incident with the Parkray, I tended to agree. The house was relatively large, isolated and very inconvenient to run. Additionally, although for the most part Mrs Westwood was mentally very alert, she did seem to have muddled patches and if she were to fall and hurt herself, she could go unnoticed for hours, even days if Alison was away. I think Mr Kemp hoped that I would be there for three weeks and get the ball rolling in that direction. However, when I tackled the subject, because apart from anything else I had to let the agency know how long I was going to be there, one week was definitely all that was necessary. When I tentatively mentioned three weeks (which is the maximum that, as a helper with the agency, we can stay

at any one time) as being the appropriate time Mrs Westwood looked at me as though I was mad — it was not going to take her three weeks to recover from a bout of pneumonia. Finally, we compromised on two weeks and I rang the agency to let them know.

Our conversation had obviously quite galvanised Mrs Westwood because she announced that she wanted to go to the hairdressers. She thought that she would feel a great deal better if she could face, with some equanimity, what she saw in the mirror. I was instructed to telephone the hairdressers who said that they would fit her in whenever she wanted and we decided on that afternoon. There was no doubt about it when Mrs Westwood said "jump" the whole village jumped!

Meanwhile the agency rang with details of my next job and when I was due to start. It left me a couple of days free and I decided to arrange to go home to Wales, meet some friends and get my new living room curtains hung. How foolish to make such plans? On the way to the hairdressers Mrs Westwood tapped me on the arm and, in her most conciliatory tone, said that she thought perhaps she would like to have someone for three weeks after all and that as we got on so famously, she didn't want another strange face, so please would I stay. In the hour that Mrs Westwood was at the hairdressers I had to do some frantic telephoning to unravel all those plans.

The hairdo worked wonders for Mrs Westwood. She said she felt much better and she certainly looked it. I had thought the scarecrow type of hairstyle was normal but of course it was the result of not having been to the hairdressers for three weeks. When we got back to her house, I thought I had better live up to my challenge and tackle the subject of her sister's

funeral. Today was Thursday and the funeral was to be next Tuesday some 50 miles away. In fact, I was forestalled by being asked to find the hymn book as soon as we had taken off our coats. Apparently, the sister had not only been so inconsiderate as to die whilst Mrs Westwood was in hospital but she had failed to leave instructions for her funeral service. Having chosen the hymns and the 23rd Psalm I cautiously suggested that Mrs Westwood wouldn't want to miss singing them. To which came the rapid retort that if her sister, she was never called by her name and I still didn't know it, was so utterly thoughtless as to turn up her toes whilst she, Mrs Westwood, was ill then she, the sister, couldn't possibly expect her, Mrs Westwood, to be at the funeral. I live in hope.

Preparations for dinner that night were going smoothly when the house telephone rang. I let it ring for a while because Mrs Westwood liked to answer it herself but, as she didn't emerge from the drawing room, I answered it. It turned out to be Alison's sister who was anxious. She had called on Alison earlier in the day and found her house unlocked, back door open, dogs not there, no sign of her sister and now, several hours later, she was not answering her telephone — please could I go and check that everything was alright. I borrowed a torch from Mrs Westwood and set off down the long drive in the pitch black and pouring rain. Needless to say, when I finally arrived at Alison's house, soaking wet, she was sitting cosily in front of a blazing log fire watching the television. She had merely gone for a walk with the dogs. She apologised profusely and explained that she often doesn't hear the telephone when she is watching the television and the sitting room door is shut. She thanked me for my efforts and sent me off with a jar of homemade jam. On return I found that the

steak and kidney pie I had just laboriously made and put into the top oven of the Aga had burnt to a cinder. I was beginning to think that, like everybody else, I had made a mistake in leaving my previous and well-ordered life!

Nonetheless a routine began to take shape as I gradually got life with my aristocratic and splendidly autocratic senior citizen under control. I had two hours off every afternoon. I hadn't got any friends close by and the weather was atrocious so walks during the afternoon were an impossibility. Instead, I took to going out for the couple of hours in my car whilst Mrs Westwood snoozed happily in her armchair. I explored Warwick, which is a lovely, old, sleepy city. I had visited Warwick Castle on several occasions but had never actually been to the city. Leamington Spa proved to be a very different proposition. It is a bustling Regency town almost impossible to park in. I only went there once on my own. I managed to find a multi-storey car park which happily let everyone in, regardless of how full it was, because it was a Pay and Display nightmare. It was a bit like musical chairs, as soon as a car moved out of a space, two cars would converge at high speed from different directions to bag it. I didn't see an accident that afternoon but I did see an awful lot of frayed tempers including my own. There wasn't even a set route to circumnavigate this monstrosity, you were free to pick different routes. In all probability the designer of this particular car park spent his/her life being happily driven around in a chauffeur driven car and never had to tackle the problem of actually parking in it.

I also explored Stratford-upon-Avon. With it being so close it would have been lovely to go to the theatre and see a Shakespeare production one evening. Unfortunately, a major snag of my current work is no time off in the evening. I can

see that my social and cultural life is not exactly going to flourish!

On the day before the sister's funeral, I really felt that I was measuring up to my challenge. Mrs Westwood was beginning to think that it would be rather nice to have a day out. The funeral was to be at 2.30 pm and she felt she would like to have lunch first in an hotel nearby and make a proper occasion of it. I was just about to call Mr Kemp and tell him of the plans when the telephone rang. It was the district nurse who announced that she would be arriving shortly, as previously arranged, to give Mrs Westwood her 'flu jab. I never smelt a rat, just thought, "what a sensible precaution".

Mrs Westwood greeted the nurse with great glee and had her injection with perfect equanimity. It was only after the nurse had left that Mrs Westwood informed me that she couldn't possibly go to the funeral now because she always has a reaction to her annual 'flu jab and would undoubtedly be under the weather on the morrow.

Feeling thoroughly thwarted I put my call to Mr Kemp on hold. I fully expected him to ring that evening to see if Mrs Westwood would appear the next day. However, he clearly knew his Godmother very well. When she says "no" she means "no" and all the persuasion in the world would not change her mind. She certainly didn't feel ill the next day and for the first time since I had been there, she donned her pinafore and positively bustled round the house doing tasks like washing her hair brushes. Being so religious I presumed that Mrs Westwood believed in an after-life but she clearly was not worried about looking her sister in the eye when next they meet.

Nonetheless, Mrs Westwood and I liked each other. She

was, without doubt, one of the remaining few from a bygone era. Life has changed so much since her childhood that it must be quite difficult for her to come to terms with the modern world and she didn't really want to come to terms with it. When so many in the UK were on income support to imagine receiving a carriage clock for your 21st birthday from the indoor and outdoor staff must be what fantasies are made of. When I told her that Simon, my younger son, was spending part of his gap year before going up to university in Egypt looking after the coral reef in the Red Sea, it transpired that she had been on three trips around the world and found Cairo very smelly. Simon, incidentally, would agree with her. Mention of Nick, my elder son, skiing for his university revealed that Mrs Westwood had shied a lot (she definitely "shied" and not "skied") in Austria staying with friends. Apparently instead of shooting around one's estate as one did at home, one shied around the estate instead. However, the war had put paid to that activity and after the war the Nazis had pinched all the skis and skins — terrible people the Nazis!

Notwithstanding her very sheltered upbringing Mrs Westwood was extremely well-informed on what was going on in the world today and politically aware. She also had a social conscience. If she were a young woman today, she might well have gone into politics. Parliament would have benefitted from the experience. She was a highly intelligent woman who certainly was not backward in coming forward and articulate to boot. As Mrs Westwood so rightly pointed out, but for an accident of sex she would have succeeded her father in the House of Lords. Undoubtedly, she would have greatly enlivened the proceedings in that elevated place.

However, I'm not quite so sure how truly religious Mrs

Westwood was. Apart from her sister's funeral, she refused to go to the Advent Carol Service in the neighbouring village to meet the new Rector of their plurality, nor go to his Induction Service which was to be in her own church the following day, and she was certainly well enough to go. As a sop to her conscience, she sent me to the Advent Carol Service in her stead — well after all what do you have a helper for? I am not religious and I find the Church of England an extremely vacillating body. It should be setting some standards instead of being so politically correct. It doesn't make clear that the tenets of the Christian faith should be adhered to, which doesn't help those who are floundering. Thus, being an unwilling recipient of a dose of religion it was with some reluctance that I left the house at 6.15 pm on a truly horrible evening to drive through pouring rain to the next village some three miles away. It is amazing how often things that you really are not looking forward to turn out to be a success. The ancient church was small and very simple. The service was by candlelight and the six, deeply recessed windows were full of white candles in all shapes and sizes. It was very beautiful. There was no choir and the organ was incredibly wheezy but the congregation sung with gusto and the readers read with feeling. I was really glad I had gone, my views on the Church of England as a whole haven't changed but that sort of service is English village life at its best.

I was coming towards the end of my stay with Mrs Westwood and she suddenly realised it. Feeling very much better, you would actually be hard pushed to realise that she had ever been ill, she announced that she wanted to go Christmas shopping in Leamington Spa and we would go that afternoon. I was delighted to be of assistance although a little

bit wary of returning to Leamington. By the time we returned I would have happily spent all afternoon playing musical cars in the Pay and Display car park to the way we actually spent it!

Mrs Westwood insisted on directing me to Leamington. This meant going via every sleepy village that she could think of and took me twice the time it had a few days previously. I was reduced to a paroxysm of coughing when Mrs Westwood sat in the passenger seat and complacently said that nobody knew the neighbourhood as she did, she knew every shortcut. She did have the merit of directing me to a car park that I managed to park in straight away but it was quite a distance from the shops. Off we set, Mrs Westwood armed with her stick and me the shopping bags. The stick was less an aid for walking and more of a weapon to prod poor unsuspecting pedestrians who got in her way. I found myself developing the habit my sons used to adopt with me when they were little and we were out shopping — pretending that they were absolutely nothing to do with me.

We went into Boots first and my heart quailed when I saw the length of Mrs Westwood's shopping list and it completely plummeted when I realised that I was going to have to get her up the escalator. On she marched waving her stick in front of her but miserably failed to march off when she got to the top. I was behind her and literally had to pick her up by her armpits and lift her off before either she, and her stick, put the escalator out of action or she did a serious injury to herself. Undeterred by the incident Mrs Westwood proceeded around Boots like a ship in full sail. My shopping bags got fuller and fuller. She didn't buy one new hot water bottle, she bought three just in case! Finally, we arrived at the checkout. Mrs Westwood paid

by cheque and was greatly affronted when asked to produce her cheque card. In an extremely loud voice, she turned to me and boomed, "my dear there was a time when everyone in Boots knew me and I have never yet had to produce my cheque card". If she had been my mother I would have shrivelled up with embarrassment, but she was not my mother so I managed to grin cheerfully at the very startled or amused faces around us.

We went to Smiths next because Mrs Westwood needed a refill for her Sheaffer biro. Now most people go up to the stands and choose the appropriate one from the rack. Not Mrs Westwood, up she marched to the checkout desk and ordered the young man attending it to find her a refill. Amazingly, he obligingly did, from a rack right at the end of the store. Having brought it back Mrs Westwood decided that she needed two refills. So back went the young man to get another. On his return it was plain to see that his patience was wearing thin and, just when a fairly low opinion of his customer flitted across his face, Mrs Westwood smiled sweetly and thanked him so much for all his help. The young man was completely disarmed! I don't suppose he had met too many Mrs Westwoods in his life.

However, Mrs Westwood was not yet ready to pay for the refills. Flushed with success she instructed me to find every imaginable size and colour of envelope. Having obtained at least a ten-year supply Mrs Westwood was now ready to pay for her purchases naturally by cheque. This time I was prepared. I knew exactly where in her capacious handbag lurked the Coutts bank card and I had every intention of diving in and producing it before I had to incur any further embarrassment. I should have known I would be embarrassed

before we even got that far. Mrs Westwood had made her cheque out to 'Smiths' and when the cashier politely asked her if she would put WH before the word Smiths and Limited after she protested, loudly of course, that everyone knew that this shop was just Smiths, it had always been just Smiths. I was beginning to come to the conclusion that Mrs Westwood hadn't actually been out shopping in Leamington or anywhere else for a very long time.

We left Smiths, Mrs Westwood still marching but less quickly and beginning to use her stick more as a walking aid and less as a weapon and me staggering under the weight of three full shopping bags. I was hoping fervently, and for a variety of reasons, that we had finished the shopping not least because we had already walked a long way from the car park and I was anxious about Mrs Westwood's ability to walk back. However, we had not finished and a box of chocolates remained on the list. So we set off further down the Parade to find Thorntons. Unfortunately, Thorntons had transformed itself into a knick-knack shop selling mainly Christmas decorations. It did, in fact, sell a selection of chocolates but nothing measured up to Mrs Westwood's requirements. The helpful sales assistant suggested that Mrs Westwood might like to go to Marks & Spencer as they stock some delicious chocolates in their Food Hall. My cup of embarrassment was not yet full, Mrs Westwood assured the assistant that she had never been in Marks & Spencer in her life, one simply did not go to Marks & Spencer! Nonetheless we did and Mrs Westwood's eyes fairly popped out of her eye sockets when she saw the Food Hall and came out clutching an enormous box of assorted chocolates. Correction, I came out clutching an enormous box of chocolates and three bags of shopping.

Having made all the purchases on her list Mrs Westwood's energy suddenly dissipated and she was down to a very slow, limping walk. It took a long time to get back to the car park and in the end, I had to hold all the shopping in one hand and support Mrs Westwood with the other. When we finally reached my car the hand which had been carrying the shopping was totally numb. The fingers were bright red and the palm dead white. It looked a bit like a piece of Blackpool rock and it took me some time to reinstate circulation.

Naturally, Mrs Westwood insisted that we return home by the same circuitous route, which was all very well but it was now dark, Mrs Westwood got confused and we got lost! Oh, the joys of Christmas shopping! However, once we got safely home it was all worth it, especially as I knew that there wasn't enough time left to embark on another shopping spree.

On my last night Alison invited us to dinner. She had bought a duck in the market on her way home from her daughter's farm and she thought I might like a night off from cooking. Alison really was the loveliest person. Her home was cluttered and comfortable and her two dogs roamed at will. We had such a merry evening. It was not so much a night off from cooking that I appreciated but someone else to talk to. Mrs Westwood was enormously interesting but she didn't indulge in idle chit-chat so after several weeks of keeping my brain on red alert it was very pleasant to be able to sit back and relax whilst Alison kept us all amused.

I thought that Alison was going to have to be fairly firm with Mrs Westwood and limit the extent of her goodwill as a neighbour, otherwise she was going to end up running both homes and effectively become an unpaid housekeeper. I was mortified that I had failed miserably to live up to Mr Kemp's

expectations of me. I didn't get Mrs Westwood to her sister's funeral and she was still determined that she can live on her own. Mr Kemp had every right to be concerned but as the old adage goes, "you can take a horse to water but you can't make it drink". Mrs Westwood was undoubtedly going to miss me and she had, at least, accepted that she couldn't drive her car any more. This, of course, made difficulties in getting to the neighbouring village where she shopped and had her hair done. Naturally, she didn't envisage a problem. She had already made a hair appointment and of course, "Alison will be only too pleased to take me in". I have warned Alison and suggested that a taxi might be the answer, but it was important that Alison started as she meant to go on. I had become fond of Mrs Westwood, she has many endearing qualities, but she has been accustomed all her life to people running around after her and she saw no reason why that should stop now. Moreover, I am not sure that she actually gave it a thought, simply expected it as her God-given right!

During my stay I had become friendly with all the shopkeepers whilst doing Mrs Westwood's shopping and in particular the butcher. He was delighted when I told him that Mrs Westwood had decided to give up driving, a few more lives saved he reckoned. Apparently, she was absolutely lethal in a car. He asked me if the car had been sold and when I told him that it was still in the garage, he suggested that I sabotage it so that she could never drive again. The butcher was quite sure that all her good intentions would go straight down the drain the minute I had left. After such a happy dinner with Alison, and fully conscious of her plight as the helpful neighbour, I lay awake all night wondering if I should creep down and put sugar in the petrol tank — the only way I know

of putting a car out of action. In the end I decided that I really couldn't go round committing acts of criminal damage even if the act was intended to prevent an accident — what a moral dilemma!

I left the next day with a degree of sadness. My initial anxieties and the difficulties experienced in undertaking something so completely off my radar, had slowly lessened and I had come to grips with what was required to be Mrs Westwood's helper. Having spent the last 20 years looking after first toddlers and then teenagers I had become accustomed to being in charge. However, no-one was 'in charge' of Mrs Westwood and she had opened my eyes as to some of the skills a helper needed to possess and if lacking them should rapidly acquire. My next job was with a disabled gentleman who had just come out of hospital after an operation. Clearly this would present a new set of issues and problems to be overcome and skills rapidly to be acquired.

Mrs Westwood was, herself, sad to see me go and I promised to call if ever I was in the neighbourhood. Regrettably her car was still in full working order and I left with the niggling suspicion that Mrs Westwood would think it an unnecessary expense to order a taxi when she had a perfectly good car in the garage. I also smiled because I'm quite sure that if, in her youth, Mrs Westwood had become a Member of Parliament she would have ensured that the Statute Book included a law preventing doddering old fools from driving!

# CHAPTER 2

I would have liked a few days in Wales to recharge my batteries after the recent three weeks but financially I wasn't in a position to turn down work from the agency so, with a feeling of tiredness, I set off for Herefordshire and Mr Forrester.

My information from the agency was that Mr Forrester is a spastic paraplegic, a physical disability that he has had since he was born. In fact, his disability is not the reason he needed my help, on the contrary I soon discovered that he was a very independent gentleman. However, he had just had an operation and his sister, Mrs Clibery, who has been looking after him since he came out of hospital needed to return to the bosom of her own family in Lewes.

Mr Forrester's house was, not surprisingly, a bungalow, and the door was opened by an amply proportioned lady with a jolly, booming laugh who I assumed, rightly, to be Mrs Clibery. As I entered the small hall Mr Forrester appeared from his bedroom with the aid of a Zimmer frame. I am not quite sure what I had expected Mr Forrester to look like, I hadn't really conjured up a mental picture, but the reality took me by surprise. I was confronted by a slight man in his early seventies, with a pleasant intelligent face, balding on top and wearing the most startling sweater. It was in navy and fluorescent red bands and had AUSTRALIA in white written all over it and there were also a few kangaroos and koalas

thrown in for good measure, so that I was in no doubt as to where the sweater had originated. I'm afraid I simply couldn't stop myself from blinking. Fortunately, introductions were made and I managed to recover myself.

As instructed, I had arrived at mid-day so that Mrs Clibery would be able to get back home to Lewes before dark. So once I had got my bag in from the car we sat down for lunch which consisted of a bowl of delicious homemade soup, bread and cheese. In order to open conversation Mrs Clibery asked me where I was from. I told her that currently I was based in Wales but, although for the last 20 odd years I had lived near Liverpool, my sons had gone to Malvern College so I knew this part of the world quite well. Mr Forrester was delighted. Apparently, he had also attended Malvern College and it transpired that he had been in the same house as Nick and Simon. It really was a small world and we had managed to break the ice very successfully.

After lunch Mrs Clibery departed taking her jolly, booming laugh with her. Mr Forrester then promptly announced that he was a poor conversationalist and wanted to be as independent as possible. My brother's words about interminable boredom came rushing back. Here I was all psyched up to bustle around the kitchen preparing tasty meals and provide sympathetic care for an ailing convalescent, whereas the reality was a charming man who had lived on his own for 10 years with a very organised way of life and who didn't want someone else in his kitchen — operation or no operation. Additionally, his disability in no way hindered his ability to manage. I was amazed at the speed with which he could zoom around the house with his Zimmer frame. Apparently, he normally managed with two sticks but during

his stay in hospital he had developed enormous blisters on his heels and couldn't wear proper shoes which made the use of sticks dangerous.

I swiftly realised that Mr Forrester just needed someone to hover in the background and do the few tasks that he couldn't yet do, like hang out the washing and do the shopping, whilst he eased himself back into his normal routine. My first evening I spent reclining on a very comfortable sofa in an elegant, albeit freezing sitting room (what is it with the elderly and central heating) reading my book whilst dinner was cooked for me. At 6.45 pm I heard the zoom of the Zimmer frame and my host, patient being the last word to describe him, appeared with an aperitif for me. Mr Forrester was a retired accountant, but he also had other talents amongst which was wine-making, and he now offered me some of his own homemade plum wine which rejoiced in the name of "Jerk 'em". That's probably not how it is spelt but that was how he pronounced it and I felt that it was too early in our acquaintance for me to enquire why it had such an extraordinary name. Nonetheless it was delicious and I am sure extremely potent.

Dinner was for the most part also delicious — grilled gammon served with damson pickle, which was the dregs of his homemade damson brandy so again thoroughly potent — but the pudding was a disaster. Charles, by now all that potency had got us onto Christian name terms, proudly told me that every night he had sago because he was very good at cooking it. I have always maintained that I can eat anything but now I realised that this wasn't true, I absolutely loathe sago. All those dreadful meals at school when we were forced to eat sago, or frog's spawn as we called it, loomed before me

and I felt sick. Sick or not, I had no option so I glued on a brave smile and ate the pudding very quickly. I even managed to compliment Charles on its excellence. However, what I really felt must have been written all over my face because in the week that I was there we never had sago again!

I soon came to the conclusion that Charles's talents might well have been misplaced as an accountant because he would undoubtedly have made a marvellous chef. He cooked dinner most nights and each was superb and my only task was to buy the ingredients. In the main I was only permitted to boil his egg for breakfast and make the soup for lunch. However, even boiling his egg put me in a nervous twitch because, predictably, he was very precise about how he liked it. When cooking Charles paid enormous attention to detail and one night made a truly gorgeous pudding called Flummery. Apparently, a cook at one of the house parties he had attended in his youth used to make it and he had obtained the recipe. It was a froth of raspberries, egg white and jelly and was as light as air. I was quietly relieved that Charles didn't have to taste my attempts at cooking much. I thoroughly enjoy cooking but for the last decade my standard has been at the level of producing as cheaply as possible vast quantities of food for a large, but indeterminate number, of hungry youths and their girlfriends. Although, when required, I did produce more up-market dinner parties for Alan.

Staving off the boredom was a problem so I decided that a bit of discipline was required. Normally my day would be filled trying to do five jobs at once, as quickly as possible and probably not very well. I had to make myself do everything slowly and immaculately. The first morning I found I had nothing left to do by 10.00 am. Breakfast was finished and

cleared away, Charles's dressing changed, the washing done and out on the line, I had even done my exercises — a token gesture to ward off the flab in my now rather sedentary existence. I was even beginning to miss the dreaded Parkray, at least I had been kept so busy I didn't have time to think! In the end I decided that I could be of most help out in the garden and spent the rest of the morning sweeping leaves. My thoughts were in a turmoil as I swept. "I really am mad, here I am bored, of not much assistance to Charles and doing a job that at home I would avoid like the plague."

I think my courage began to dissipate marginally at this stage. One friend had told me that frequently the devil you know is better than the devil you don't. All I knew was that currently I felt like a new girl on her first day at boarding school and I hadn't enjoyed that much either.

After lunch, whilst Charles was resting, I went for a walk along the canal. It was a beautiful, crisp afternoon and my spirits lifted. I came across a wonderful old church and, buoyed up by experience at the Advent Carol Service, I went in. Sadly, I was too full of conflicting emotions to find any peace. Instead, God, if there is one, got an earful. If he had intended marriages to work why did he make men such sods! My walk didn't really help much despite its auspicious start.

The next day I decided that my couple of hours off, whilst Charles was safely tucked up in his bed having his rest with his Zimmer frame discreetly hidden, were going to be put to good use. I have some great friends who live in a pretty market town just half an hour down the motorway. In fact, they own the local hotel. A quick call and "yes" they would love to see me however briefly. Praying that the motorway would be clear (I may not entirely believe in God but that didn't stop me from

frequently offering up fervent prayers) I should be with Anthony and Gilly by 2.30 pm which would leave me time for an hour's chat and be back in time to make afternoon tea.

I was greeted with great warmth, lots of hugs and kisses and a large glass of Beaujolais Nouveau (still some left from the recent run to France to get it) was thrust into my willing hands. Life definitely began to look a great deal better. I told Anthony and Gilly about my experiences thus far and we all had a good laugh. Time flew by and it was with horror that I looked at my watch and realised that I was going to be very late. Drinking and driving was hopefully not going to be a problem — I had only had the one, albeit large, glass — but producing Charles's tea on time was. With more hugs and kisses I was on my way again sending up an even more fervent prayer that the motorway would still be free.

Actually the 'first day at school' syndrome soon disappeared and I positively began to enjoy myself. Despite maintaining that he was not a great conversationalist I learnt much about Charles. His divorce, his three children (the youngest of whom lived in Australia, hence the sweater), his childhood and the problems he had faced with his physical disability. Even more surprisingly I discovered that he was something of a spiritualist. He showed me this beautiful crystal on a fine gold chain and told me that when he was troubled, he consulted it. He explained me that he held the chain so that the crystal hung unmoving and straight down. He then closed his eyes, concentrated on the problem worrying him, asked a specific question and opened his eyes. If the crystal started to swing backwards and forwards the answer to his question was "no". If the crystal started to swing round in a circular motion the answer was "yes". I obviously looked somewhat

incredulous because Charles laughed, handed me the crystal and suggested that I try it later when I was on my own. I did. It was quite extraordinary. I asked two questions. The first "had I done thing right thing in leaving Alan" received a definite "yes" and the second "should I go back to Alan" received a definite "no". Rationally I told myself that I had probably unconsciously influenced the answers and only time would tell if they were correct but it was an interesting experience and I certainly looked at Charles in a different light.

The evenings were a problem to begin with. Charles hardly watched the television and he didn't have any videos. I am an avid reader of books but it was difficult to settle down to a cosy read in a room that seemed to be only just above freezing. With all his innate good manners Charles asked me to put on the electric fire if I felt cold, but as this was situated directly behind his chair I didn't like to. He would soon have expired from heat and he didn't need another spell in hospital. To solve the cold problem, I took to sneaking off to my bedroom just before aperitif time and putting on a vest and a T shirt under the polo neck sweater and heavy-duty sweater I was already wearing.

Deliverance is always at hand, so I am told, it would just appear that you have to know where to look for it. Charles mentioned that he played bridge regularly. Obviously, you can't play bridge with two people but if he was a card player then the chances were that he had some other games lurking in the house. Sure enough, he had cribbage and bezique. I knew how to play cribbage so it was fairly inevitable that Charles chose bezique which I had never even heard of.

With a sinking heart I set up the card table and my heart sank even further when I was handed a book of instructions on

how to play Royal Bezique which was printed in microscopic proportions. The one guaranteed aspect of middle age is that your eyes begin to deteriorate and my problem is that I am not prepared to admit that I am middle aged and, therefore, there is nothing wrong with my eyes. Consequently, I don't possess reading glasses. I embarked on that game of bezique not having a clue how to play it. Charles obviously decided that I needed some outside assistance and produced a bottle of damson brandy which was truly delicious. Two glasses of that and two games later I began to get the hang of how to play. We spent a very merry evening and the brandy not only improved my card playing skills but also successfully kept out the cold. For the rest of the week, we spent every evening playing bezique and swigging the damson brandy with just one brief break to watch *Casualty* on the television. The episode we watched for me was déjà vu. An extremely expensive power boat went aground and the occupants nearly drowned. The scene was meant to be located on the south coast but I recognised the scenery and it was actually filmed in my part of Wales. It was rather curious seeing your home depicted as somewhere else and more glamorous to boot. We never normally saw powerboats of that dimension and opulence.

On Sunday Charles asked me if I would like to go to church. I didn't, but I said "yes" because I assumed that he wanted to go and would need me to drive him. By this time, I had discovered that he was on the Parochial Church Council and was, in fact, the treasurer. However, it transpired that, despite an incredibly speedy recovery from his operation, he didn't feel quite up to it but of course I had now committed myself so, with some reluctance, I set off.

During the week I had met both church wardens who had

come to visit Charles and enquire after his health. One was a delightful old farmer and the other a very pleasant young woman. The church was at the end of an extremely narrow lane with old farms on either side. I had driven because it was pouring with rain and I parked at the end of the line of cars outside the church. As it happened it was not only family service but a baptism as well. The church was full and the only vacant seat I could find was in the middle of the nave. I sat down and the parents and the baby had just arrived when the delightful church warden came down the aisle asking, in a voice like a foghorn, who owned the blue Ford Fiesta because it was blocking the milk lorry. With a face as red as a beetroot I slunk out of my seat and the church with every pair of eyes riveted on my back. Having extricated my car and endured the wrath of the milk lorry driver I didn't resume my seat but remained firmly at the back of the church. I was tempted not to return at all.

The service went without any further hitches and the baby, Bethany, was as good as gold. Afterwards coffee was served to the congregation which I had intended to miss except that the dear old church warden, I was beginning to have serious doubts with regard to his delightfulness, collared me and asked me to wait whilst he counted the collection so that I could take it back to Charles. It was difficult then to refuse a cup of coffee and I stood feeling rather spare in a crowd where everyone quite obviously knew everyone else but worse was to come. I had just finished my cup of coffee when it was whisked out of my hands and two large bags of money placed there instead. Once again, every pair of eyes was riveted on me and I could just see the thoughts, "what on earth was a total stranger doing with their collection?" With my face again as red as a beetroot

I launched into a long and garbled explanation as to who I was, and why I had their money, to anyone who cared to listen. I then left the church very quickly.

Sunday night, which was my last, was also the night when I was going to be allowed to cook dinner, a roast. Knowing the standard that had been set, not being overly conversant with electric ovens (at home I have an Aga) and the roast being beef with Yorkshire pudding, I was naturally nervous and that was the understatement of the year!

However, perhaps because of my second bout of holiness in a short space of time, God was on my side and all went well. We really made a festive occasion of it and had the best china, a bottle of wine and conversation flowed freely.

Once again, I was really quite sad to leave the next morning after breakfast. Looking after Charles had been quite different to looking after Mrs Westwood, my tally of necessary skills had grown and I had enjoyed the experience.

A big kiss and a merry twinkle of his bright blue eyes and I went on my way.

# CHAPTER 3

After leaving Charles I went back to Wales for a few days' respite. It was bliss to be able to lounge about in bed in the morning drinking endless cups of coffee and reading the newspaper, simple pleasures but such luxury. I got my new sitting room curtains hung and they made a huge difference. Having been a summer holiday home, until now we had never done things like drawing curtains (the sitting room is on the first floor overlooking the sea) and it is amazing how important they are in the winter. The place had seemed very cold and cheerless when I first moved in but now with a lick of paint, new curtains and lots of plants it was a joy to come back to.

Unfortunately, the joy was short lived. Alan wanted a meeting to discuss things and my heart sank. We agreed to meet halfway for lunch. I felt that if we were in a public place Alan would, at least, have to control his temper. He was looking well, handsome as ever and he said that he was very glad that I had agreed to meet him — so far, so conciliatory.

"We'll just have a chat like old times," he said smiling, and he had such a charming smile that I was almost disarmed, but not quite.

"Hardly like old times, old times recently were mainly a screaming match remember," was my tart reply.

"Well let's talk about your work," Alan countered.

So I told him all about Mrs Westwood and Charles. He

held his head on one side and appeared to be taking it all in and enjoying my narration. Thus, it was like being hit in the solar plexus when he said slowly and carefully, "don't you think it is all a bit demeaning?"

I just stared at Alan and even he began to look uncomfortable but, having started to dig his hole, typically he continued digging. "Surely you must realise that my wife should not be acting like a menial servant, I think it best if you come home. Please can we try again".

If he had started with his last sentence, and never said the rest, I might have been tempted to consider a return. Although I had come to enjoy my time with both Mrs Westwood and Charles I had already begun to wonder if I could actually be a helper for the rest of my life. But the rest of his words acted like a focus in binoculars, everything became clear. Alan was used to getting his own way. Alan was used to being an important and respected member of society. Alan was used to having a compliant, decorative wife who managed his home life smoothly, appeared with him when required but otherwise did as she was told. Alan was not used to having a wife who had not only left him, but had left him to undertake work (in his opinion) of a very menial nature, and his ego had suffered a massive blow.

I stood up, gave Alan what I hope was a withering look, turned on my heel and left the restaurant without another word.

I returned home in tears, all my resolve to be independent had dissipated with every mile. Not knowing what else to do I telephoned my elder son, Nick, and he restored both my sanity and my resolve in a long chat. Four pieces of advice from Nick clarified my thoughts: firstly, hadn't I thought long and hard about leaving Alan and why I was leaving Alan; secondly had

anything changed to currently alter that decision; thirdly being a helper was not demeaning work, far from it, it was work to be both applauded and respected; and fourthly I had two sons who both applauded and respected my decision and fully supported me in whatever I decided to do. It was definitely worth persevering through all that adolescence and statements in life to make, to end up with such a kind, intuitive and sensible son.

So suitably buoyed up I prepared for my next job, which up until then, I had been viewing with some trepidation. Mrs Hartnett, according to her nephew who had made all the arrangements, is a widow of limited means, in her 90s suffering from the onset of Alzheimer's and requiring 24-hour care and constant watching. I wasn't sure that I could cope with Alzheimer's but after my recent chat with Nick I was put on my mettle. I was to be with her for Christmas so it would be a very different Christmas from usual.

Christmas was normally frenetic with the mafia gathering from all corners of the country. Stockings had always been the best bit of Christmas because we had those at home, but the large family lunch will be missed only with heartfelt relief. Last year, as my contribution, I was detailed to organise smoked salmon eats to go with the champagne before lunch. This I did, and our branch of the family duly arrived at the mafia headquarters for the festivities at 1.00 pm as previously instructed. Having provided the canapés I had imagined that I wouldn't be involved any further in the catering arrangements and, as a result, had put on my brand new and very expensive red Jaeger dress — very Christmassy. When we arrived, we found all the 22 guests assembled in the drawing room quaffing champagne and my smoked salmon was greeted with

glee. The only person missing was one of my sisters-in-law and I surmised that she must be in the kitchen. It struck me as slightly unfair that no-one was helping her so I drifted off to see what was happening. In the kitchen I found my sister-in-law with one enormous cooked turkey and literally nothing else cooked at all. In fact, she was just starting to chop up the onion to make the bread sauce. The roast potatoes hadn't gone into the oven because the turkey was so huge there hadn't been room. The two Christmas puddings hadn't been started and even in a pressure cooker they take two hours. There was nothing for it but to roll up the proverbial sleeves and help. The first task was to get the turkey out of the oven and the potatoes in. I couldn't find an apron and I couldn't find any decent large spoons or even a large fork so it was fairly inevitable that whilst transferring the turkey from the roasting tin to the carving dish hot fat spilt all over my beautiful new dress. My sister-in-law had abandoned the bread sauce and had started sipping champagne instead whilst watching me with some amusement. When asked how we were going to keep the turkey hot my sister-in-law merely shrugged her shoulders and continued sipping. I resorted to tin foil and towels. In the end the sister-in-law resumed her role of cook and between us we had Christmas lunch on the table in just over an hour. The rest of the mafia, having spent that time quaffing champagne, were in a very benign mood. This year I would happily settle for an oven-ready canary for just Mrs Hartnett and myself.

Doris Hartnett lives in a very dilapidated bungalow in a quiet cul-de-sac and wasn't actually at home when I arrived. Every Tuesday she went to the local care home for lunch and this was the only occasion when her helper had any time off and I had appeared on Tuesday lunchtime. My heart

plummeted to rock bottom when I was informed of this by the pleasant Australian that I was taking over from. Helpers were supposed to have a full day off a week and ostensibly two hours off each day, only it was recognised that this was not always possible. The thought of being tied to this cheerless house for three weeks, with only a weekly respite of two hours, was enough to depress even the most cheerful of souls, and after my few days in Wales, despite Nick, I was still not really feeling that cheerful.

Cheery Australian left, well leaving would make her cheery, and I immediately telephoned Mrs Hartnett's nephew who had made all the arrangements but apparently was never seen. He airily announced that his Aunt's helpers never had a day off but that he was quite willing to pay for the days in lieu. I felt like telling him, just as airily, that in which case he could find himself another helper but I knew that the agency had no-one else to send, and with the bills in Wales forever hanging over my head, the extra money would come in handy. So I politely thanked the nephew for his generosity. I think my sarcasm went straight over his head so I thought it best to point out at this stage that he was going to have to pay me double for Christmas and Boxing Days. He made no demur and you could almost feel his relief down the telephone that he had solved the problem of his troublesome Aunt for the festivities.

I was beginning to wonder what Mrs Hartnett was like. My telephone conversation with her nephew revealed that I had to ring the grocery order through to his wife's shop and it would be delivered. In the meantime, I was not expected to go to any other shops. Certainly, Mrs Hartnett was not to be allowed to do any shopping. I felt more as though I was to be her gaoler rather than her helper.

Mrs Hartnett was duly returned by a worker from the care home. I rushed out full of enthusiasm and introduced myself. I was rewarded with a frosty look from the worker and a blank stare from Mrs Hartnett. It later transpired that everyone at the home was concerned that Mrs Hartnett was collected from one helper in the morning and delivered back to a different one. Since July Mrs Hartnett has had a different helper each week so no wonder she was muddled and confused.

Having got Mrs Hartnett into the house I decided to start the introductions afresh and we agreed that I should call her Doris and she would call me Hannah although in reality she rarely remembered my name except first thing in the morning. I had never met anyone with Alzheimer's before and was not sure what to expect. I only know that they have little, or no, short term memory and that eventually their memory goes altogether. Doris was a fairly plump lady with a kindly face, short straight grey hair, glasses and didn't look anything like as old as 93. She was very upright and mobile and she also had a leg which was heavily bandaged.

The cheery Australian had left me some notes on Doris's routine and when she had to have her pills and eye drops, so having chatted for a bit I made her a cup of tea and duly administered her first medication. The array of pills and drops was enormous and I only hoped that I would manage to give them to her in the right order. Taking the pills considerably upset Doris for no particular reason. So to distract her I asked her if she would tell me about herself. This, fortuitously, was a good idea. Doris brightened and launched into her life history. She was the only child of a railway worker and his wife. There had been a little boy but he had died in infancy. Doris had obviously had a happy, although rather lonely,

childhood and then she had never had any children herself despite being married twice. Her first husband had been a decorator and, as she told me with a wry smile, "we had the wedding and my parents had the honeymoon". Apparently, mother and father, having got their only daughter married, sailed off immediately to South Africa to visit some relative, leaving Doris and her brand-new husband to mind their house. When the parents returned a year later the husband died of cancer and Doris was a widow. There is no doubt life really can be a downer. Although being a dressmaker by trade Doris, being newly widowed and wanting to escape her parents' house, went to work as a housekeeper for an engine driver on the railways. Stories sometimes do have happy endings. Doris married her engine driver and for the next forty years she devotedly sent Ted off every day with his sandwiches and billy can to boil up on the fire in his engine — he drove the last of the steam engines. They lived happily in a railway cottage but never had any children — their only sadness.

What floored me was having told me about her life with enthusiasm, she suddenly became very agitated because Ted would be getting anxious about her. She had left him on the corner of the street and he wouldn't know where she was and would I please take her home now. She had seemed so rational. I managed to get over that hurdle by suggesting another cup of tea but the rest of the day dragged slowly on with depression settling over me like a blanket. I would never survive three weeks!

After supper, which we had at 5.30 pm, I suggested turning on the television. I am well into the Australian soaps. As teenagers the boys always watched them so I have become indoctrinated. In fact, in Wales all water sports stopped at 5.00

pm and my house was invaded by a large number of dripping boys and girls who then sat glued to the television and consumed all my biscuits. It was only after I had turned the television on that I realised that Doris's eyesight was so poor that she didn't even bother to look at the set, in fact her chair had its back to the television, she just listened. So I took to choosing programmes that would be interesting from her point of view. Drama was difficult for her to follow but she enjoyed humour. When we watched a recording of the *Two Ronnies* on Christmas Day she practically fell off her chair laughing at their jokes. She had a lovely sense of humour herself and was naturally a very jolly, happy person but her loss of memory, which came and went, confused and distressed her.

That first evening Doris mainly dozed in front of the fire but I caught her looking incredibly sad and when I asked what was the matter, she said she didn't know who I was, or where she was, and she wanted to go home. There is no doubt that the constant stream of helpers was not helping her confusion one bit.

After putting her eye drops in, a major feat in itself as she had four different sets of drops, two for each eye, I tucked her up in bed. I then firmly wrote 'left' and 'right' on the eye drops to ensure that I didn't do irreparable damage to Doris's eyes by muddling them up, locked the back door and pocketed the key. I had been warned that Doris had a tendency to wander. I hardly slept a wink that night in case she did. I would have felt happier if I could have tied a piece of string from her big toe to mine then I would have known instantly if she got up. In fact, Doris was always as good as gold at night. From the moment I said "good night" she never moved a muscle until I said "good morning" with her cup of tea the next day. The

book of instructions informed me that Doris liked her helper to have an early morning cup of tea with her so I duly took my coffee (I'm not partial to tea) in as well. There was nowhere to sit except the bed, which was a large, old-fashioned double bed on a wooden frame and covered with a wonderful, great big, pink eiderdown — no duvets for Doris — so I sat on the corner of that and we drank our early morning cuppas.

That first morning Doris still had no idea who I was so I made her repeat my name and I did that every day. However, she was quite happy to tell me the history of the eiderdown. It had been made for her parents by her Aunt Florrie who was, "as awkward an old maid as you are ever likely to meet but handy with a needle."

The eiderdown had always lived on her parents' bed and she had loved playing in it as a child. There is very little wrong, as yet, with Doris's long-term memory. Her parents' meeting was straight out of Upstairs Downstairs. Her mother had been in service and, as a new parlour maid up from the country in a large house in London, she had nowhere to go on her one day off a month (and here am I going into a decline because I don't get a day off a week). The cook, called Polly, took pity and whisked her off to her Aunt and Uncle for the day and their son was detailed to walk the young parlour maid back in the evening. Love blossomed and Doris's parents duly got married and lived happily ever after. Somehow, it seemed to me that, despite all modern progress, life today was more stressful and less contented and divorce more prevalent.

Doris's life was actually remarkably busy and my initial despondence was not long-lived. Two days a week Heather, the home help, came and she certainly beat me when it came to verbal diarrhoea. Once a week the auxiliary nurse came to

give Doris a bath and I have to confess I was glad that that task was not expected of me. Doris was of quite chunky proportions. Once a fortnight the hairdresser came to make her look glamorous and she did. Having her hair done worked wonders for Doris's well-being and she positively preened herself in front of the mirror, which was quite out of character as she was normally very modest and self-effacing. On Thursdays we went to Reading. A coach took, for free, any old age pensioner who wanted to go to Reading. It left at 9.30 am and returned at 11.30 am. It was a marvellous service and Doris and I always took advantage of it. There must have been about 40 souls who went and they were a lovely group of people who delighted in seeing a young face — well everything is relative!

It was on the first coach trip that I discovered how Doris had hurt her leg. Whilst waiting at the bus stop a splendid, little, old lady called Dulcie came up to us, wagged her finger in Doris's face and told her that today she was not to think that she was Tinkerbelle in Peter Pan. Doris, of course, hadn't got a clue what she was talking about and so couldn't enlighten me. When the coach arrived, the driver looked first in delight at seeing Doris, delight that she was out and about again, then his expression changed to one of horror and he pleaded with Doris to use the steps in the coach this time and not try to fly down them. It didn't need much imagination to realise what had happened.

The coach dropped us right in the middle of Reading. Doris and I would potter and do her little bits of Christmas shopping. I bought some expensive Christmas crackers for Nick. He was spending the festivities in the Alps as he had to be there immediately after Christmas to train and compete in

the university ski races. Probably not high on his list of things to take but as far as I am concerned Christmas wouldn't be the same without those silly hats and ridiculous jokes. I also bought some crackers for Doris and myself. Simon probably didn't want crackers. He would be spending Christmas in Egypt, and in some style, with the parents of his great school friend, Mark, who was working with him on the coral reef. In fact, it was Mark's father who had organised the jobs for them. The conservation of the reef was a project being undertaken by the EC along with other organisations and Mark's father was with the EC delegation in Cairo - crackers would probably be de trop.

Each time we went to Reading I took Doris into a café for a cup of coffee. She was like a small child on a treat and it gave her the greatest pleasure. Although Doris couldn't see much, I finally discovered that she was totally blind in her right eye, she loved to hear all the noise, the chatter and the laughter. On our way back in the coach one old dear always handed round a bag of sweets so we would munch our way home and everyone was happy. Dulcie, in particular, was a hoot with a wicked sense of humour. She described herself as one of the monkey tribe but to me she looked more like a dormouse and we became good friends.

Dulcie and I may have hit it off immediately but it took me sometime to form a rapport with Doris. However, she gradually came to know who I was even in her confused moments. The most distressing aspect of Alzheimer's would appear to be that the victim knows that their memory is going and finds it hard to cope with. Most of the time Doris would be quite alright and then suddenly everything would go blank but frequently afterwards she would realise what had

happened and it upset her dreadfully. She had very little short-term memory.

After several days we were getting on like a house on fire and Doris seemed infinitely better, less confused and more alert. I encouraged her to read the paper which she had delivered every day — *The Sun*. Despite her poor eyesight she could still read, but because it was fairly difficult for her, she just didn't bother. To keep her occupied I suggested that she read out loud to me whilst I was preparing lunch. She spent twenty minutes reading to me all about the Prince and Princess of Wales' separation and adding her own comments on the subject at the same time. Mrs Westwood would have approved of her viewpoint! I was just congratulating myself and writing off the entire medical profession for not really understanding Alzheimer's and how best to cope with it, when Doris picked up the paper again and exclaimed, "Well I didn't know that the Prince and Princess of Wales are separating". My apologies to the medical profession!

Nonetheless we did make progress. My greatest joy was when I went in one morning with her tea together with my bright, "Good morning Doris," and she replied, equally brightly, "Good morning Hannah". She said that every morning for the rest of my stay. However, I also had my dramas with her. I swiftly discovered that she really did wander. I had been so careful in the house but taking her out was another matter. One morning we went in my car to post her Christmas cards. When we got to the Post Office Doris decided that it was too cold to get out and she would stay in the car. We were parked right outside the shop so I just got out and popped in. Unfortunately, there was a large queue of people all wanting to post their Christmas cards so I patiently

joined the end. It never occurred to me that Doris would disappear. I had left her perfectly happily in the front seat and she still had her seat belt on. By sheer chance I glanced out of the window whilst waiting and to my horror saw that my car was empty. Outside there was no sign of Doris and I had no idea whether she had gone to the left or the right. For a moment I simply froze but then realised that this was no time to dither. I ran as fast as I could to the right. My luck was in and I caught up with Doris just as she was about to cross the road. I was shaking like a jelly. Her eyesight was so limited that she could hardly see the kerb let alone an oncoming car. My imagination had her either, dead by falling over the kerb and fracturing her skull or, dead from being hit by some poor unsuspecting motorist. Fortunately, today was one of her good days and she recognised me and was quite happy to go with me but, "we really did have to get to the railway because she had forgotten to give Ted his sandwiches and billycan". Needless to say, every time we went for a trip in the car after that I put Doris in the back seat and locked the doors. I wouldn't put it past her to attempt to bail out when we were actually driving. When she became confused, she was completely unaware of her surroundings.

Housekeeping for Doris also exercised all my organisational skills. I had never before had to live on £54.40 a week which was the old age pension and it was a salutary lesson. I had retained a few nice thoughts about the elusive nephew because, even if he never came to see his Aunt he was, at least, paying the bills. However, when a letter arrived from a solicitor about the Power of Attorney and another one from the Abbey National Building society about Doris's savings, I realised that she was in fact paying all her own bills and her

money was not going to last forever. Therefore, it stood to reason that the less I spent each week out of her pension on food and household necessities the more there would be left over for the electricity and telephone bills, etc.

Washing was a major chore. Doris didn't have a washing machine, only an antiquated spin dryer, so everything had to be washed by hand. Fortunately, there was another wonderful neighbour, Jane. Wonderful neighbours were obviously destined to be my lifesavers. Once a fortnight Jane put the double sheets and big towels in her washing machine which was an enormous help. There then only remained the snag of how to get them dry. It rained most of the time I was there so hanging them out on the line in the garden was out of the question. On my first morning with Doris, I was confronted with four wet double sheets, two wet long bolster cases, four wet pillow cases and two wet gigantic towels, no possibility of drying them outside and no handy radiators to put them on as there was no central heating. I found a very inadequate piece of string strung across the kitchen and one small clothes horse. I had to dry the washing by instalments, it took me the best part of a week and the kitchen permanently looked like a Chinese laundry. The first time I used the spin dryer it tore around the kitchen like a headless chicken so I abandoned that as an aid to washday. I began to think that it was extremely lucky that I had been brought up on a farm where, when we first moved in, there had been no electricity, the water had to be pumped up from a well and the washing all went through a mangle! I used to love operating the mangle. I have to add that we finally achieved all mod. cons. but my early experience was now standing me in good stead.

Nonetheless I had never been confronted by a whalebone

corset before. Doris held her stockings up with an impressive girdle which was anchored together with a long line of hooks and eyes. When I decided it was due for a wash, I couldn't find a replacement. Her drawers were full of quantities of undergarments but not another girdle. The only thing I could find was a whalebone corset complete with laces. It was going to have to suffice. Unfortunately, inspection showed that the laces were broken and quite clearly not up to the task of containing Doris's ample figure. I put off washing the girdle and we made a visit to the village shop. This shop had no pretensions to being a country version of Harrods and could only offer me black trainer laces, so fetching with pale peach, but in any case, would not have been long enough. I bought many yards of white tape and went back to effect repairs.

The next day it took me ten minutes to get Doris into the corset and I just prayed that the tape would be strong enough to hold it together. When it came to actually attaching the stockings, I discovered that one of the suspenders was minus its tab and therefore useless. Doris was not in the least put out "just fetch me a button and I will fix it" was her calm suggestion. Easier said than done. I ransacked the bungalow and found cotton, needles, scissors in abundance but no buttons. Obviously, there were some but finding them was the name of the game. Eventually I unearthed an old shoe box full of ancient tobacco tins. These revealed the most amazing collection of buttons. Armed with several in different sizes I returned to Doris who was still sitting patiently on the bed and smiling sweetly. In a trice she had dextrously attached her stocking to the suspender with a button.

The whole episode could have been somewhat embarrassing for Doris (she is normally quite capable of

dressing herself but this was beyond her) but Alzheimer's certainly has not affected her sense of humour. Whilst struggling with the laces to the corset she and I were laughing so much that I thought I would never complete the task. Tears were literally running down Doris's face!

I would just love to know how previous helpers had coped with the fact that Doris only had one girdle, perhaps they didn't think that a girdle needed washing. In any event I decided that the next time we went into Reading I would buy her a new girdle in Marks and Spencer but when I saw the price of a girdle, I realised that Doris's pension would not run to it, not with the Christmas presents she wanted to buy, or rather the presents I was reminding her she ought to buy. It crossed my mind that I could buy it and give it to her for Christmas but I didn't think Doris would be too impressed when she opened her present. The chances are she wouldn't remember the incident, despite its hilarity, and a girdle is, under normal circumstances, a fairly uninspired present. In the end I decided my only course of action was to warn the next helper about the dilemma. In fact, further perusal of the tobacco tins revealed some spare suspenders so I was able to fix the corset. Nevertheless, my successor was still going to have to shoe-horn Doris into this amazing piece of memorabilia!

Doris was undoubtedly looking forward to Christmas. It was interesting that she did retain certain things and every day she knew that Christmas was coming without any reminders. Usually, a card or two would come through the post which caused great excitement. She didn't want to have a Christmas tree. Curiously, she had never had one and perhaps that was because she had not, as she described it, been blessed with children. At this time of year some mothers might described

their children as mixed blessings.

The run up to Christmas became positively hectic. Lots of people popped in to see Doris, many bringing gifts with them so that her pile of presents grew. She was just like a small child, she got so excited. An added excitement was the day a very sizable cheque came through the post from Ted's old regiment's welfare fund wishing Doris a Happy Christmas. Her eyes sparkled and she sent me straight out to buy a bottle of sherry so that we could celebrate Christmas properly. I wasn't going to disagree with that sentiment. One caller who came was the most enormous woman I have ever seen. She was so large that she couldn't sit in the armchair by the fire but had to sit on the sofa. There was no doubt that this particular friend of Doris was definitely winning her battle against anorexia!

I also had my visitors. On the day that Doris went to the care home I met a great friend, Penny, who was on her way from Liverpool to London, for lunch in a pub. It was wonderful to relax, have a drink and catch up with gossip. The hot bit of gossip being that I had been seen walking on the beach in Wales with my dog looking simply wonderful and I quite obviously had a lover. My reaction was instantaneous — chance would be a fine thing! The rumour was unlikely to survive because anyone who knew me and Alan also knew that the dog in question, a spaniel, was firmly on the pheasant shoot at this time of the year and not strolling around beaches in Wales. We exchanged Christmas presents and as mine felt like something to wear I couldn't resist opening it as soon as I got back to the bungalow. It was the most gorgeous multi-coloured Paco rugger shirt. My spirits instantly soared — I love good friends.

I didn't confess to Doris that I had opened one of my presents because I was being very bossy about not letting her open any of her presents until Christmas Day.

Nick came to visit me before setting off for the Alps. Because his life was so busy, he couldn't make it for my free lunchtime so with a little trepidation I invited him for lunch at the bungalow. Doris had happily agreed to Nick's visit but I was worried in case she had forgotten about it resulting in the visit upsetting her. I spent all morning reminding Doris that Nick was coming so when he was rather late arriving (nothing new there, he'll probably be late for his own funeral) she tartly told me that, "a watched pot never boils," as I lurked by the window keeping an anxious eye on the drive.

Doris and Nick hit it off immediately, mainly because she exclaimed with delight on meeting him, "what a handsome young man". We had wine with lunch and, apart from Doris telling Nick that she was only here on a visit herself, everything went swimmingly. I also opened Nick's Christmas present to me, well out of Doris's vision. It was a really splendid Filofax. I was absolutely thrilled and now felt more like a high-powered executive than a helper. My presents to him and the crackers joined the Christmas tree in the back of his truck along with his skis, boots, guitars and the myriad bits of equipment. A big hug and kiss, and then he was off. It was so lovely to see Nick and seeing him depart made feel really sad and homesick. I was going to miss him and Simon dreadfully at Christmas but, I consoled myself, I would have missed them even if I had been back in the bosom of the mafia — they both were always going to be away this Christmas.

All that afternoon Doris talked about Nick's visit but I must confess that the glass of wine featured most prominently

in her chatter. At lunch, the next day she wanted to know if we were going to have wine again. It made me laugh but for Doris it was an exceptional piece of memory retention. There was no doubt she could remember exciting occurrences and clearly a glass of wine rated alongside Christmas in terms of excitement. I was beginning to think that I could do with a dose of Alzheimer's myself. I could then remember all the happy occurrences in my life and conveniently forget about the disasters.

On Christmas Eve Doris and I went to the Carol Service in the local Methodist church. Predictably Doris was a deeply religious soul. I was definitely getting the impression that someone, somewhere was taking a hand in trying to convert my atheist views. It was a lovely service held by candlelight. We all held candles which looked beautiful but made finding the carols in the book and actually reading the words a trifle difficult. It was bad enough for me but impossible for Doris. It was with some acerbity that she told the rather ineffectual minister, as we left, that if God had seen fit to invent electricity why revert to candles! I just smiled placatingly.

Christmas Day dawned with great excitement and present opening. Doris's face was a joy to watch. I had bought her a pink lamb's wool cardigan and she was thrilled, rubbing it gently against her face with a smile of pure delight. In the middle of the morning, after we had been to church — again, we had a surprise visit from the elusive nephew, David Lewis. In fact, I was already beginning to review my rather negative opinion of him. He was actually no blood relation to Doris but was the great-nephew of Doris's late husband. Mr Lewis also has a brother and sister, neither of whom did anything for Doris despite possessing the same relationship and only living

five miles away. Mr Lewis had a disabled son, Patrick, who came with his father on the Christmas visit. Apart from having two more children, his recently deceased father's farm and his own garage to run, Mr Lewis was the 'special needs' governor of two schools and Chairman of the Parish Council. Obviously an extremely busy person.

Mr Lewis and I had a long chat about Doris and her future. The agency was very expensive and only provided temporary help, hence the change of helpers on a frequent basis. A permanent carer would be difficult to find as Doris's bungalow was so small and there was the ever-present problem of time-off, or the lack of it! In the end we decided that a care home would probably be the best solution. Doris was so frequently confused about her surroundings that it was unlikely that she would miss her home and the constant companionship of others would be stimulating for her. She dearly loved a chat and a laugh. As Patrick and his father left, I made a mental apology to David Lewis, elusive he may be, but he was doing his best to ensure that Doris was properly cared for.

Boxing Day was a hoot! The wonderful neighbours, Jane and Neil, invited us round in the evening to join in their family get-together. Neil's sister, husband and two children were there plus Jane and Neil's own son and daughter. The young were all great fun and in their early twenties. We had an enormous meal followed by a card game called Aintree which I had never heard of before. Everyone produced piles of pennies and I realised that we were into gambling in a big way. I just wished that I had brought Doris's purse as well as my own. It was a simple game not requiring much skill but we had an hilarious time. Doris and I didn't seem to have too much luck with the cards but every time we did manage to win some

pennies she was overjoyed. When, very late in the evening, I persuaded Doris that it really was time to stagger home next door, otherwise we would never make church the next day (typically Sunday fell immediately after the festivities), everyone donated their pile of pennies for the collection.

So, on Sunday I was back in church armed with yet more bags of money! By now I have surely earnt my place in heaven! This time I managed not to blush when Doris told the minister, who was still being ineffectual, that the money was her gambling winnings — he was completely nonplussed! Frankly, he would have been even more amazed if he had realised that for Doris to remember her misspent evening at all was a remarkable feat. Once more I had every pair of eyes in the church riveted on me.

My time with Doris drew to a close. When the new helper arrived, I spent ages filling her in with details of Doris's routine and foibles. The woman clearly thought that I was either mad or I seriously doubted her intelligence. I hadn't meant to be bossy but Doris had made such progress in that she appeared far happier and more contented than when I had arrived and it would be nice if she could stay that way. Ultimately, I was sure that a place in a care home was the long-term answer.

# CHAPTER 4

A change at last! I was beginning to think that I was destined to spend my entire time looking after the elderly which, as I have discovered, can be tremendously rewarding but I was looking forward to rather more youthful company for my next assignment. Furthermore, I was going back to the part of the world where I grew up — Surrey.

I was off to Chiddingfold to look after, by the sound of things, a very harassed husband and two small girls whilst his wife was in hospital having her gall bladder removed. Mrs Chadwick had my heartfelt sympathies. I have had my gall bladder out and it was a particularly unpleasant experience.

My instructions were precise, well Mr Chadwick was a management consultant so he should be able to manage my safe arrival even in the dark, and I easily found the narrow lane that led out of the village and up to a beautiful but rambling Tudor farmhouse. The Chadwicks owned the house and a paddock but the rest of the farmland had been sold to the local potato farmer, an extremely successful potato farmer apparently. I was never entirely convinced, by the farmers' moanings about the EC and the dire state of farming in England. I had yet to meet a poor farmer and they all seemed to drive around in Range Rovers, BMW convertibles and Mercedes. In fact, coming to the Chadwicks down the narrow lane I had met a Range Rover, most likely driven by the potato farmer, who was oblivious to the fact that there simply wasn't

room for two cars to pass. He had simply come roaring towards me with his foot on the accelerator and headlights blazing. I had only one option and that was to take to the hedge as fast as I could and my language had left a lot to be desired!

It was about 9.30 pm when I arrived. On leaving Doris I had returned to Wales and had managed a lovely long telephone conversation with Simon in Cairo. He was ecstatic about diving in the Red Sea and keeping all the tourists off the coral reef. He had found Christmas a little strange but had enjoyed it nevertheless and he was really looking forward to spending New Year's Eve trekking around the pyramids on a camel! I was very relieved to know that he was so happy and well. However, no sooner had I finished the conversation than I received a phone call from the agency. It was clear that Mr Chadwick was feeling quite desperate and needed help without delay. It would also appear that there were no doting Grandparents in the vicinity who could help out in a time of crisis, or just help out full stop. It was a long way from Wales to Surrey hence my late arrival but at least I had arrived.

Mr Chadwick proved to be a pleasant man in his early thirties whose huge relief at seeing me was immediately apparent. It always irritates me when women describe themselves as "just a housewife" and I am driven berserk if a man describes his wife in that fashion. Being a housewife and a mother is hard work, requires great organisational skills, is frequently deathly tedious, sometimes chaotically hectic but there is nothing "just" about it! Certainly, Mr Chadwick was not a dab hand at being a "househusband". Peter, we got onto Christian name terms the minute I stepped through the front door, had taken a few days off work to cope but my first glance in the kitchen indicated that his talents were obviously better

suited to the field of management consultancy. There were toys all over the place, mounds of dirty clothes on the floor in front of the washing machine, more mounds of what were presumably clean clothes in a wash basket looking horribly wrinkly, piles of dirty dishes on the draining board and, despite being fairly late in the evening, there were still a huge variety of cereal packets on the kitchen table. Peter did have the grace to look apologetic and trying not to look too superior I assured him that I would have everything under control in the morning.

Both girls, Emily and Sophie aged five and three, were in bed so Peter took me into the lovely big sitting room and we sat in front of the enormous inglenook fireplace, had a whisky and got acquainted. Apparently, Peter and his wife, Rosemary, had only moved into the house a year ago and during all that time she had been having bad attacks with her gall bladder. So, what with that and two small children to look after, not much had been done to the house and much needed doing to the house — like installing central heating! I think I stand a good chance of developing pneumonia. I had gone from the heat of Mrs Westwood's house, courtesy of the famous Parkray, to the cold of Charles's and now to near arctic conditions in Surrey. My brother is probably feeling very smug at this moment. Much as I love him, he is one of those irritating sorts of people who is always right!

Peter gave me a quick guided tour of the house which was big, and it was hard to orientate myself, but I felt that I would look forward to exploring it in the morning. Peter then showed me to my bedroom, announced that he had written out the girls' routine, pleaded for his breakfast at 7.00 am and departed hurriedly before I could protest, ask any question or even weakly say "yes".

Feeling fairly gobsmacked (an expression frequently used by my sons when they were younger) I sat on the bed which felt wonderfully warm. Thank goodness for electric blankets and thank goodness that Peter had had the foresight to turn it on. He probably wanted to ensure that I didn't do a moonlit flit. A brief perusal of the typewritten pages I had found on the bedside table — Peter's secretary probably enjoyed typing this little document — revealed that the girls were early risers, time unstipulated, and ate enormous breakfasts. Emily had to be at the primary school in the village by 8.45 am and Sophie needed to be at her play group in the neighbouring village three miles away at 9.00 am. Sophie finished at 12.30 pm and Emily at 3.15 pm. Rosemary was to be visited with Sophie in hospital in Guildford some 15 miles away. I could see that I was going to be roaring around Surrey at high speed in order to be in all those places at the right time. I just hoped that I wouldn't meet too many farmers in Range Rovers!

I didn't bother to unpack my bag. I felt my order of priority was to get a good night's rest if I was going to be able to tackle tomorrow. I set my alarm for 6.30 am, kept the electric blanket on and drifted straight off to sleep.

I needn't have bothered with the alarm. My bed was a splendid old fashioned one on legs and stood about three feet off the ground. In the morning I was woken by what sounded like mice scrabbling under the bed followed by a loud whisper of, "shush you will wake her". It would appear that my two little charges had crept in to see what the helper looked like. As soon as they realised that I was awake two adorable, fair-haired girls scrambled onto my bed. They were bubbly souls only too ready to tell me anything and everything and didn't seem the least wary of this stranger in their midst. In fact,

Emily confided in me, with a world weariness more suited to a 50-year-old than a five-year-old, that she was glad that I had come as looking after Sophie and Daddy was hard work. I think Daddy would have been horrified to hear those words as he was obviously under the misapprehension that he, Peter Chadwick, was the one doing the looking after!

To my horror I saw that it was only 6.00 am. The typewritten routine had not specified how early was 'early rising' and I had forgotten what hyperactive creatures, small children can be. As I was wide awake, I decided that I might as well put the time to good use and unpack my bag. Emily and Sophie proved willing helpers and were overcome with admiration at the photos of Nick and Simon. Both boys are products of their time and have long hair, Nick's being down to his shoulders and blonde and Simon's is dark and curly. Emily thought that they looked like popstars and Sophie agreed, although she probably had no idea what a popstar was. Nick would have been delighted as being a popstar was high on his list of possible careers and he was actually quite an accomplished guitarist and lead vocalist. However, at the moment he was safely tucked up at university, or at least I sincerely hoped he was. I have long since stopped being complacent about what my children might be getting up to but, to date I had no information that they were not where they should be, and I work on the premise that "no news is good news".

Unpacking completed I thought it best to supervise the girls dressing before going downstairs to tackle the kitchen and breakfast. It was a good idea. Emily's dressing was quite straightforward as she had to get up in her school uniform. However, Sophie left to her own devices would have chosen

the most improbable combination of clothes and put them all on upside down and inside out, well she is only three. The girls each had their own bedroom next door to one another. Bright, cheerful rooms but in much the same state of chaos as the kitchen with yet more dirty clothes scattered everywhere. God was receiving another fervent prayer about the reliability of the washing machine. As far as I could see it would be working non-stop for the two weeks that I was to be there. The arrangement was for Rosemary Chadwick to be in hospital for another week and then I would spend a week with her here to help her on the road to convalescence.

Downstairs breakfast was quite easy to prepare because most of the ingredients still lingered on the table from yesterday. I merely cleared sufficient space for four places, found enough clean china and cutlery to lay them and we were there. It transpired that no-one ate a cooked breakfast. The only requirement after cereal was vast quantities of toast, marmalade and jam. Emily took her responsibilities very seriously and it was she who solemnly informed me of the family's eating habits. Although I was already feeling slightly jaded, I think Peter was pleasantly surprised to arrive down to find the day under control and three smiling faces. He was looking very business-like and handsome in an immaculate pin-striped suit. Being in his own metier suited him and the rather hunted look had gone from his eyes. It was with a definite quirk of humour that he wished me luck as he surveyed the kitchen before departing for more high-powered business. The typed timetable informed me that he would be back at approximately 7.00 pm if I was lucky!

I didn't attempt to wash up before taking the girls to their schools. I was anxious about finding them and I certainly

didn't want to be late. Emily's school was easy to find as it was in the village and she was able to direct me, but Sophie's playgroup had to be found down three miles of narrow, twisting, totally confusing lanes. I knew from experience never to rely on country signposts as they rarely point in the right direction. However, as invariably happens if you set off in plenty of time everything goes smoothly. It is only when you set off late that life goes from bad to worse. Thus, I arrived at Sophie's playgroup ten minutes early. It was a bitterly cold day so we sat in the car and played some cassettes. Unfortunately, Sophie wanted Thomas the Tank Engine and all I could offer her was La Traviata or The Magic Flute. I made a mental note to put some of their own tapes in my car.

With the children safely delivered I returned to the farmhouse to tackle the chaos. I hadn't under-estimated my abilities, I am pretty capable at restoring order. Nonetheless it was by sheer chance, and with horror, that I glanced at my watch and discovered that it was 12.15 pm. Sophie needed collecting from playgroup, I had done nothing about her lunch and we had to be at the hospital by 2.00 pm. Grabbing my handbag and a handful of the girls' cassettes I set off looking like the wreck of the Hesperus and feeling like it as well. As I tore along the lanes, the potato farmer was lucky not be on the roads as he would have been no match for me that morning, I did some rapid thinking. With the lack of lunch prepared I simply would not have time to do that and get us to Guildford in time to visit Rosemary Chadwick in hospital. I hoped Sophie liked chips. It transpired she did, most children do. However, Simon didn't and so I could have been caught out. Sophie and I had a happy lunch in the car park of Guildford hospital munching the chips I had bought from a nearby fish

and chip shop and listening to the tape of The Three Billy Goats Gruff. I debated on whether to warn Sophie not divulge either the venue or the menu for her lunch to her mother, but on balance decided that such a warning would probably guarantee that Sophie's greeting would be rapidly followed by lurid tales of chips in the car. It was bad enough lying in bed, feeling decidedly unwell without having to worry that your enormously expensive helper was feeding your children on a completely unbalanced, cholesterol chocked diet. The enormously expensive bit is, of course, relative. To me it was not enough and I had constant niggles as to how I was going to pay all the bills for the house in Wales, including the infamous Council Tax. However, to a young couple with two children, a mortgage and a house in need of renovation it was a lot of money to be shelling out.

We found the ward quite easily and Sophie was overjoyed to see her mother. Rosemary Chadwick is a pretty woman, or I am sure would be in normal circumstances. Today she looked very wan and dejected. The fact that her hair needed washing didn't help. Nonetheless she produced a smile when we met and insisted that I call her Rosemary and said how relieved she was that I had arrived. Sophie chatted happily and avoided any mention of chips. I spent the entire visit on tenterhooks, ready to dive in and steer the conversation into safer waters if necessary. Rosemary filled me in on the family's culinary likes and dislikes, those that Emily had missed, and where to find various things in the house.

As we left to make the mad dash to pick up Emily, Rosemary plaintively asked if I would bring some shampoo with me tomorrow and a hairdryer. I decided to add some games to the list in order to keep Sophie amused the next day

whilst I gave Rosemary a hand with her hair. Gall bladder operations involve drains and tubes, all of which makes hair-washing a difficult and tiring task.

We got to Emily's school on time and I was really feeling quite pleased with myself and my efficiency. I should have realised that puffing up one's own ego inevitably means that it will very soon be deflated. As Sophie and I stood outside the school gates one of the mothers, who clearly knew Sophie and the fact that Rosemary was in hospital, asked me if I was the girls' Granny. I know that I had had a busy day. I know that I hadn't had time to brush my hair or put on any lipstick but did I really look like a Granny? That hairdo obviously had more to answer for than I originally thought. I not only looked dowdy I also looked old. The poor girl was covered in confusion when I icily told her that I wasn't Sophie's granny. I was tempted to leave her to crawl out of her predicament by herself but finally decided to take pity on her. After all it wasn't her fault that my hairdresser had misinterpreted my instructions. I followed up my coldness by gently suggesting that it was an easy enough mistake to make as I was in charge of Sophie and waiting to collect Emily. It was a wise move. Anita and I subsequently became great friends and have remained so ever since. During the time I was with the Chadwicks she frequently came to tea after school with her two little daughters, Laura and Kate. The four girls were good playmates and got along well most of the time except for one incident. Laura, for whatever reason, decided to pull Sophie's hair which threw the afternoon into a scene of complete hysteria. Being the mother of two sons, hair pulling was not something that I had come across and I was at a loss as to how to deal with it. My initial instinct to pull Laura's hair just as

hard was clearly not the answer! In the end I resorted to appeasement — how about tea with cupcakes and jelly — it did the trick!

That first afternoon, however, the friendship hadn't flourished and so to run off a bit of their surplus energy I decided to take the girls for a walk finishing up at the village shop to do some basic shopping for tea and dinner that night. Kitted out in wellies and anoraks we set off. Originally Sophie insisted on carrying the shopping basket but her little arms weren't long enough and the basket trailed in the mud. Since I still had several days cleaning and washing remaining in the house, and didn't need the extra hassle of a dirty basket, I took over.

We walked across the adjoining farmland which wasn't all put down to potatoes. One field we came to was full of cows, only they didn't look like cows to me but suspiciously more like bullocks. I am terrified of bullocks. I was once chased on our farm by a herd of bullocks as a child. The fact that they scared the life out of me was only made worse by my father roaring with laughter at my terror and assuring me that they had only wanted to play. When I ran, they ran, for them it was a game. Needless to say, I was not reassured. Now looking at the field of bullocks I was still not reassured. I think Emily must have sensed my anxiety because she took my hand and solemnly told me that the cows wouldn't chase us. Clearly a near-granny can hardly let herself be outfaced by a five-year old girl, so over the stile we went and walked along the edge of the field. Sure enough, up came the bullocks but only at an ambling pace. Resisting the urge to run I looked them in the eye and marched, albeit with a thumping heart, onwards. Sophie asked me if they were for sale. I hadn't got a clue and

rather bewildered wanted to know what had prompted the question. With enormous patience (I was beginning to get the feeling that there was a bit of role reversal going on between the children and myself) Sophie replied that, "if they are not for sale why have they got price tickets in their ears?"

Sure enough, each bullock had a metal tag clipped to the edge of his ear, presumably for some form of identification. It occurred to me that the Hon Mrs Westwood might have met her match with these two young ladies. It would be interesting to see who came out the winner after twenty minutes' repartee, certainly it would be a close-run thing.

We made it safely to the shop and bought the necessary provisions. Fortunately, the Chadwicks had a slate there because I had forgotten to ask Peter for any housekeeping money and I had very little cash on me.

The girls had sausages and beans for tea, I got through some more washing, persuaded the unwilling souls to clear up their toys, gave them a bath and by the time Peter arrived home they were in their pyjamas in the sitting room watching television and looking angelic.

Peter was undoubtedly impressed, but then I think they had been living in such bedlam since Rosemary went into hospital that even the slightest improvement would have impressed him. Emily and Sophie obviously adored their father and I left them playing happily whilst I went to prepare dinner.

The kitchen was the one room that the Chadwick's had already spent some money on. It was large and with a low oak-beamed ceiling. There was an oil-fired Aga but also an electric oven and grill and an electric hob. The dishwasher, washing machine and tumble dryer had all been built into the units

which were oak fronted — no more shrouds, thank goodness! The wood was beautiful and the workmanship obviously that of a craftsman. The units were large and plentiful and remarkably well ordered. The chaos in the kitchen may have looked mind-boggling but was, in reality, only skin-deep. It was a warm, attractive room designed to have much time spent in it.

The village shop didn't stock a large range of groceries so I had settled on spaghetti Bolognese and a salad followed by cheese and biscuits. To be honest I really hadn't got the energy to cook anything more elaborate. Unquestionably small children were far more exhausting than the elderly but that did have the advantage of leaving little time for dwelling on personal problems. Although I was going to have to do some dwelling before too long. Alan had completely disregarded our recent disastrous meeting and was still convinced that my insanity was only temporary. He made it quite clear in a brief telephone conversation that he was expecting me to return — oh the arrogance! I had promised Nick and Simon that I wouldn't do anything irrevocable in a hurry but at some stage I was going to have to make some definite decisions.

Dinner was an enjoyable meal. Emily and Sophie were tucked up in bed and, although I fully expected it, we didn't have any interruptions from them. Peter was good company and I began to think that maybe all men weren't such sods, just a selected few. He was very concerned about Rosemary and he told me at length about his plans for the house. It was a very long-term plan. Despite a good job, once all the day to day expenses had been met there was not much left over for improvements. Nonetheless, Peter had great vision and judging by the job that they had already made in the kitchen,

one day the house would not only be beautiful but comfortable as well.

I was beginning to realise that it was always the first 24 hours in a new job that were the most hectic but I was also developing a sixth sense as to where to find things in strange surroundings. Life with the Chadwicks soon developed into a busy but happy routine. The children and I got on well and they got on well together with only a minimum of bickering, although Sophie strongly objected to being used as a colouring book. I had left the girls playing in Emily's room whilst I did some cooking. Emily was colouring a picture using a large array of felt-tip pens. Feeling faintly anxious about felt-tip ink appearing on the walls, floor, doors, etc., and unable to persuade Emily to do her drawing in the kitchen, I sternly warned her that the room must stay pristine clean. I had a splendid cooking session in the kitchen whilst blissful quiet reigned in the house. This peace was shattered by outraged shrieks from Sophie. I rushed upstairs to find that her face, arms and hands were covered in a mad, lurid design of felt-tip ink. Apparently, Sophie had been perfectly happy to participate in this activity until Emily had finished and she, Sophie, had looked in the mirror. We had to endure even louder yells from Sophie when I put her in the bath and attempted to scrub Emily's handiwork off. It actually took days before I finally managed to remove it all. Notwithstanding this furore Emily was most affronted when I ticked her off for her behaviour. She had not drawn on the walls, floor or door and I had never mentioned Sophie's anatomy in the dire warning. It was very taxing trying to stay one step ahead of bright young girls!

The family seemed to enjoy my cooking but I am sure

Peter thought that I was a pretty scatty cook. About the only time that he came into the kitchen whilst I was earning my pay was a disaster. Feeling a bit lonely in the sitting room he had strolled into the kitchen with his drink for a chat, just as I was making soup. My mother would be proud of me, she always thought me fearfully extravagant. Ever mindful of the Chadwicks' strained finances I had taken to making soup out of all the odds and ends. I never threw anything away and when I had got enough bits, I fried some onion and garlic in a saucepan, added the bits and some stock, boiled them for a few minutes and then threw the contents into the liquidiser. The result was amazingly tasty soup. Well on this occasion I had failed to attach the top of the liquidiser properly and when I turned it on would be home-made soup sprayed all around the room hitting everything in sight, including Peter who was happily sipping his whisky and water. His pin-stripe suit was no longer so immaculate and I expected that most of my wages would go on paying the cleaning bill but he did, at least, laugh. In fact, we both laughed a lot and it was good to see Peter looking less stressed even if he was splattered with soup!

Life became considerably more difficult when Rosemary came out of hospital. It is always tricky having two women in the same kitchen and, apart from feeling decidedly under par, I think Rosemary resented the easy, friendly relationship I had developed with Peter and the girls. After a week spent being merrily in charge and bossing everyone around, I had to start walking on eggshells.

The first evening Rosemary was so pleased to be home that she accepted the dinner that I had prepared with great pleasure and pronounced it delicious, but unfortunately disaster (another one) struck that night. We had all gone to bed

and presumably asleep, certainly I was, when the night was rent asunder by screams of anguish. Sophie was quite obviously having a nightmare. I rushed out of bed and into her room at exactly the same time as Rosemary rushed out of hers. I let Rosemary pick Sophie up, although after major invasive surgery she shouldn't have been picking anything heavy up, and I put the main light on. A week is a long time in a small child's life and for the past week I had been the person to comfort Sophie in her times of trouble. Consequently, Sophie continued to howl in her mother's arm and on seeing my hovering person she howled for me. I felt for Rosemary, no-one feels their best in the middle of the night, one feels even worse when recovering from major surgery and one feels completely suicidal when your child rejects you. Between us we quietened Sophie but I reckoned that the incident did not augur well for future relations and I was going to have to be the soul of diplomacy, a task I am particularly unsuited for.

Next morning Rosemary stayed in bed whilst I did breakfast and the school run. She had been fairly frosty when I had taken in her breakfast on a tray and when I arrived back at the farmhouse, I am afraid the thaw had not yet set in. It was a difficult situation because there was nothing really for me to apologise for in order to make her feel better. She had just got to rationalise the situation in her own mind. It was a weary morning. Fortunately, the day's schedule was so busy there wasn't time for the situation to get out of hand.

As the week progressed Rosemary gradually began to feel better and relations between us definitely improved. Peter took advantage of my presence to stay at the office late into the evening in order to catch up with the work that he had missed and so, once the girls were in bed, Rosemary and I frequently

found ourselves curled up in front of the wonderful inglenook fireplace.

It was during one of these evenings that I discovered the reason for the lack of grandparental help. Both Peter's parents were dead. He had a married brother but he lived in the wilds of Scotland. Rosemary's parents were divorced. Apparently, it had been a particularly acrimonious divorce. Although her parents hadn't actually divorced until Rosemary was 18, they had separated when she was 13. In the intervening period there had been mistresses galore on her father's side, perpetual hysterics or deep depression on her mother's and no money for anything but her sister's ponies. Rosemary had had to ride as well to look after her younger sister but it was not something that she was keen on and certainly was not very good at. Being a keen horse rider myself I couldn't easily relate to Rosemary's lack of enthusiasm with regard to horses. Her relationship with her mother had never been good. Frankly, it sounded to me as though 'Mummy' was thoroughly spoilt, selfish and self-centred. The relationship deteriorated completely when Rosemary married Peter. The lack of parental money meant that Rosemary had to pay for the wedding herself. Daddy had by then remarried and was not in the least interested in paying for anything let alone a wedding. The family home had been sold and the proceeds divided up during the eventual divorce so Mummy was in rented accommodation. The only light in this gloomy saga were the truly marvellous paternal grandparents and the wedding reception was to be held at their house. You would have thought that Rosemary's parents, albeit divorced, might have been pleased that she had saved so much and was able and willing to fund the whole wedding. Not a bit of it, all she

seemed to get was endless carping and bitterness from her mother, so much so that Rosemary came out in a nervous skin rash. She quite thought that she would have to walk down the aisle with her face and neck covered in angry, red, scaly patches. Fortunately, she didn't and despite everything the wedding went well.

However, her relationship with her mother did not improve. Rosemary may not be the easiest personality but her heart was in the right place and she was very caring. I would hazard a guess that her mother was jealous of her. Jealous of her ability, jealous of the fact that she had married a man who could give her the material things in life and who was faithful. Poor Peter was working so hard at the moment to provide those material things that I don't suppose he had either the time or the energy to stray from the fold, apart from not having the inclination. Jealousy is a very corroding emotion. Apparently when Emily was born her mother, who lived several hundred miles away, refused to come and visit on the pretext that the journey was too much for her. Thus, in order for her mother to see her first grandchild Rosemary had to make that long journey with a two-week-old baby. Having your first baby is a very emotional and rather unnerving experience, especially if you have given birth to a howler. Emily may be a lovely child now but apparently, she had been a very demanding infant. Mummy, with her usual lack of thought, had filled her minute house with stray friends and relations with insufficient beds to house them, so that at night it was a bit like walking over the bodies asleep on Delhi railway station. There was absolutely no peace, no calm and Emily howled incessantly. Poor Rosemary lasted three days (I would have given it 24 hours) and then she drove home in tears and desperation. With a

history like that I could quite understand that Rosemary, realising that she was in for a bad time medically, felt that she was unable to cope with her mother as well, even if ostensibly Mummy was doing a good turn. A fortune spent on a helper was infinitely preferable.

Having poured out her life's history Rosemary then enquired about mine. I wasn't really ready to talk about my current situation and thus gave her the bare bones. In order to make up for this paucity, and not to appear standoffish, I regaled her with my childhood and how I had been brought up on a farm not many miles away with plenty of horses which I rode daily. I told her about the fun I had had as a teenager meeting friends in the local pubs, going to Point to Points, going to the cinema in Guildford and generally having a good time. I told her about my first love, Michael. He was the epitome of tall, dark and handsome with a very infectious grin. We had met at the rugger club dance when I was 18, and it had been love at first sight. Michael had done a fine arts degree at university and was working for an art gallery in Guildford. I loved visiting the gallery and seeing the different art but of course the main reason for going was to hear Michael's wonderfully sexy voice explain the various pieces. He also had a horse and loved riding, definitely a bonus. What sealed our relationship was Michael's response when I was badly injured in a car crash. I had been a passenger in a friend's car when she misjudged a bend and went off the road. I was knocked unconscious, suffered multiple cuts and a fractured skull. When I came round in hospital there was Michael asleep, with his head on my bed and clutching an enormous bunch of magnolias, which he later told me had been nicked from his parents' garden. I may have had a fractured skull and in pain

but I had never been so happy!

At 18 I just wanted to have fun. I had no clear idea of any possible career and how I was going to earn a living. Certainly, I was not cut out to be a doctor, lawyer or any other professional and my parents finally persuaded me to do a secretarial course in London. To begin with I commuted by train every day, but having finished the course, and landed a well-paid secretarial job for an engineering firm based in Lygon Place, I decided to share a flat with three other girls who had been on my course in Kensington. My relationship with Michael, although in the first flush had seemed perfect and would last forever, unsurprisingly did not survive my move to live in London and, of course, I then went on to meet Alan. But you never forget your first love.

After that evening of revelations Rosemary's attitude to me was much less guarded and she was considerably happier to accept my help. When you are so used to doing everything yourself, it is quite difficult to delegate tasks and put up with the fact that those tasks may not be done as well as you would have done them yourself. Probably it is only if you have been brought up in the pampered existence of dear old Mrs Westwood that you are able to accept assistance with perfect ease. By the time we went shopping in Guildford Rosemary and I were the best of pals.

Rosemary was anxious about Peter's company's annual dinner dance and the eternal problem of having nothing suitable to wear. Men really don't know how lucky they are to be able to don the same old dinner jacket year in and year out. One of the snags of major surgery is that you are not supposed to drive a car for six weeks after the operation, a nightmare prohibition in this day and age, particularly if you live in the

country. So I suggested to Rosemary that she take advantage of my expensive presence and let me chauffeur her into Guildford. Off we set one morning after the school run like two children playing truant. We had got out of our uniform jeans and into our glad rags and Rosemary clutched the Chadwick credit card.

Guildford may not be the centre of haute couture but it has one or two really quite respectable boutiques. Rosemary was undecided whether to go for something practical that would also fit the bill for dinner parties or splash out and get something really glamorous. I urged her to go for the latter. She needed a creation to give her spirits a lift and my spirits certainly lifted helping her. In one boutique the poor assistant probably thought she had got two escapees from the local loony bin in her shop but really it was her fault for putting the wrong sizes on the dresses. Rosemary picked out a truly gorgeous midnight blue strapless dress with a full mid-length skirt and a huge bow on the front. The ticket on the dress was marked size 10 and so she tried it on. I think it must have been size 18! The mid-length hem actually touched the ground and as it had a stiff petticoat it stood up all on its own. The huge bow acted as a pair of weird glasses for Rosemary's eyes. We just fell about laughing and were quite uncontrollable. Between gasps I assured Rosemary that if an impact was what she wanted to make at the office party then this definitely was the dress to buy, no-one was going to forget her after seeing her in this creation. On the assistant's extremely agitated offers of help we emerged from the cubicle and promptly reduced the rest of the customers to mass hysteria. To be fair to the poor assistant she was most apologetic and more than helpful. Rosemary eventually bought a fabulous flame red dress. It was

also rather pricey but being the hardened shopper that I am I suggested to Rosemary that she just tell Peter it was a bargain and grab the credit card bill when it arrived. Once Peter saw her in that dress, he was not going to begrudge the money.

My two weeks with the Chadwicks drew to a close. Once again, we had a festive last night. Emily and Sophie were allowed to stay up, Peter came home promptly from the office and we all had an early dinner. Emily had helped choose the menu, mainly I think, to ensure that her favourite foods were on it. We had roast chicken with all the trimmings, followed by apple crumble and cream and/or ice cream. I made a prawn cocktail for a starter. Starters had never featured in the girls' young lives to date and they were thrilled at being so grown up. By gourmet standards it was a simple meal but we all thoroughly enjoyed it. Rosemary looked so much better, Peter was obviously delighted to see her that way and Emily and Sophie revelled in being allowed to stay up so late.

Next morning, I did the breakfast and the school run. It was sad saying goodbye to those mischievous cherubs and I have to confess that I wiped away a tear when I said goodbye to Rosemary but then it was on the road again. Potato farmers beware — I had no intention of getting any more scratches on my car, it had probably got to last me for years!

# CHAPTER 5

Miss Little, a blind lady of 83, I liked on sight. This liking was greatly aided by the fact that her first words to me were, "My goodness you sound much too young to be a helper". Well, she couldn't see the famous hairdo, could she?

I had arrived in Burford much refreshed after a week in Wales. It was quite an education to discover how many people take refuge in their summer houses to recover from over-indulging during the Christmas and New Year festivities. I saw lots of friends, ate well, drank even better and thoroughly enjoyed myself. Simon rang from Cairo, the camel safari had been a great success and he was definitely swiftly adapting to the luxury of life in diplomatic circles. It was the chauffeur driven Mercedes that really appealed. I would be interested to hear the chauffeur's comments on his generally scruffy appearance! The hot gossip regarding my love life had obviously spread (I have a sneaking suspicion that it originated in Wales and then shot off down the bush telegraph to Liverpool) because several people commented on how well I looked and that it must be due to all that walking on the beach! I decided to rise above all tittle tattle. My brief holiday was only marred by Alan telephoning as soon as he arrived back from his skiing holiday just to mention that he had fully expected me to be safely reinstated in the matrimonial home on his return. His arrogance and complete lack of understanding fair took my breath away but my withering look

was ineffectual in a telephone conversation and I was totally at a loss for words. We did not seem to be making much progress towards a reconciliation. Anyway, I was now destined to be in this beautiful village for the next three weeks.

Miss Julia Little lives in an enchanting 16th century thatched cottage just off the main street. The standard bumpf from the agency had provided scanty information about her, the main noteworthy items being that she didn't possess a washing machine (horrors) but that she did possess a guide dog. I was somewhat expecting a Labrador which I would enjoy taking for walks. Reality confronted me with a rather overweight pooch of indeterminate years. Bella actually was an extremely well-bred spaniel but middle age and an over-indulgent mistress had combined to disguise this fact. I subsequently discovered that a washing machine was unnecessary. Ethel, who came once a week to clean, washed all Miss Little's 'smalls' and everything else went to the laundry. Ethel it transpired has known Miss Little all her life and used to be her lady's maid in bygone days. I seem to be oscillating between one end of the social spectrum and the other.

Miss Little lived up to her name and was tiny, which was just as well because the ceilings of the cottage were very low and full of beams. I'm not very tall but even I found that I was unable to do my exercises properly. It was impossible for me to stretch my arms above my head.

Miss Little had actually only been totally blind for about nine months and was finding her blindness quite difficult to come to terms with. Although she had never worked (if you discount being a land girl during the war, which was very hard work) Miss Little had always been a very active person

enjoying her garden and long walks with the spaniels which she bred in a serious way. One of her dogs even got to Crufts. She would never forget that day. She was up at 4.00 am to catch a coach in Oxford which was to take all the hopeful Supreme Champions to Wembley, plus owners. Unfortunately, the coach broke down just outside Oxford which resulted in a two-hour delay, increasingly fractious would-be champions and their equally fractious owners. Except for Miss Little who apparently remained very calm, which I could believe as she was a very serene lady. One of the hopefuls actually won his class, which whilst thrilling for all, meant a wait of an extra hour, then two, then three for the rest of the coachload. Eventually, however, they set off only to develop a puncture on the way home. Miss Little finally arrived home at 2.00 am the following day! The whole outing sounded like a Whitehall farce which was probably why it continued to live vividly in Miss Little's memory.

Miss Little did not forget the day she went blind either, it was an horrendous experience. Apparently, the sight had failed gradually in her right eye until it had finally gone altogether but her left eye had been fine. One afternoon she came in from a walk with her dogs and thought the cottage seemed very dark, but being an old cottage with small windows this was not an uncommon occurrence. However, when she put the light on she realised with horror that she still couldn't see anything. At first, she thought that maybe there was a power cut but then she realised that even if there was no electricity, she was not in the gathering gloom but in total darkness. She groped her way to the telephone only to discover that she couldn't possibly ring her doctor as she couldn't see to dial the numbers. For a moment utter panic set in then she thought to

dial 999. Apparently, the emergency services were marvellous. They telephoned her doctor who came round immediately and had Miss Little admitted to hospital. Sadly, there had been a haemorrhage behind her retina and there was nothing that could be done to save her sight.

Her blindness created a difficult and expensive situation for Miss Little. She definitely didn't want to move into a care home. She was very independent and her brain was as alert as ever. However, her cottage was small and she didn't feel that she had sufficient accommodation to offer a housekeeper on a permanent basis so she had opted for the expense and confusion of temporary help. Thus, every three weeks Miss Little had to meet and adjust to a new voice, although she had started having repeat helpers. Unless it was a repeat helper Miss Little had no idea of the personality of the helper she was getting and some she liked and some she didn't. Nonetheless she admitted that the constant change could be stimulating. With her activities now so severely restricted each new helper offered fresh ideas and conversation and she enjoyed finding out about them. This I discovered immediately. To date I had found that at the start of a new job I was the one who had found the first chat illuminating. After a cup of tea, it was Miss Little who was very au fait with my life history and I was none the wiser about hers. Miss Little had perfected the art of gentle probing and was very inquisitive about me, why I was a helper and about my family. I never needed much encouragement to wax lyrical about my sons and obligingly I launched forth.

Tea finished Miss Little explained the geography of the cottage and how to find my bedroom which was perfect. Two tiny, deeply recessed windows just under the thatch with pretty curtains and gorgeous antique furniture. The bed was comfy,

and I'm sure aired, and I could sit there and watch the portable television or put out a hand and turn on the radio/cassette player left for my entertainment. Definitely the best-appointed bedroom I had had thus far.

Downstairs in the sitting room, where we had had tea, there was a large television but Miss Little rarely watched it because without sight it gave her scant enjoyment, although she was addicted to Coronation Street. We ate many suppers listening to the dulcet tones of Vera Duckworth! The radio was Miss Little's lifeline together with talking books. She said she blest the invention of the cassette player every day. Until you are faced with a certain disability you have no idea what is available but it would seem that the blind, are well catered for. Two organisations sent cassettes through the post, one being of selected newspapers, and the library stocked a reasonable selection of titles. The only problem was getting sufficient books that appealed to Miss Little that she hadn't already read. She was an avid listener. She had existed mainly on a diet of Catherine Cookson and Rosamunde Pilcher so I introduced her to Desmond Bagley and Dick Francis to put a bit of adventure into her life. Miss Little particularly liked Dick Francis because her brother had been one of the race starters at both Cheltenham and Ascot. Ascot was her favourite because it was in the days when the starter, resplendent in frock coat and silk topper, rode down the racecourse on an immaculate hack to start the race. Miss Little had obviously been very fond of her brother but he had sadly died. However, she still had one sister living, many nieces and nephews and even more great-nieces and nephews. Her sitting room was full of happy family photographs.

I found Miss Little a bit disconcerting to begin with in that

she firmly told me that she could eat anything and that she didn't want to be consulted about what to eat. However, she was, in fact, rather pernickety in her eating habits so until I had managed to find out, by a process of elimination, what was acceptable and what was not I lived on tenterhooks. Nonetheless I found out an interesting fact in the course of this process. Miss Little apologised for preferring plain cooking and that being such a brilliant cook I must be finding life dull. I couldn't understand why she had this notion about my culinary skills until she inadvertently let slip that this information was on my CV. The only explanation had to be that one of the friends I had asked to stand as referee must have hyped up my capabilities in order to ensure that I obtained employment instead of remaining as an emotional jelly in Wales. This snippet of information would also explain why the agency had been so keen for me to go straight from Doris to cook lunches for forty for a commercial shoot in Leicestershire. The manager of the shoot was desperate and needed not only someone who could cook but who was also socially acceptable — that was the part I liked. It is comforting to know that you are thought to be socially acceptable even if I was, in Alan's eyes, currently doing a demeaning job. I had been tempted because it would certainly have been different and might have been fun but I was looking forward to a few days in Wales — not that I got them thanks to the Chadwicks. In the light of Miss Little's revelations, I was heartily glad that I had refused. The manager had undoubtedly been expecting a Cordon Bleu cook which I definitely was not.

I debated whether I should contact the agency and suggest that they amend their computer records both regarding my abilities as a cook and Bella's pretensions to being a guide dog.

Every morning I walked up Burford's lovely main street, which even at this time of year hummed with smart, county types accompanied by Labradors and retrievers (they unquestionably had Range Rovers and Volvos in their garages), feeling slightly bashful as I trailed my snuffling, overweight pooch to buy the *Daily Mail*. However, on balance, I decided not to. I needed the work and Bella, despite her looks, was an OK sort of dog and I had become quite attached to her. The daily paper that a person took was quite an insight into their personality. Charles Forrester and the Chadwicks took the *Independent*, Mrs Westwood the *Telegraph* and Doris the *Sun*. Naturally Miss Little doesn't have a daily paper, only newspapers on cassettes, and so I indulged myself with the *Mail* — not exactly the thinking woman's paper but easy to ready and a welcome diversion.

Miss Little, in spite of her blindness, was a very keen walker, much keener than her dog. On our first outing I was very solicitous, grabbed her by the arm and set off very slowly. After ten yards Miss Little stopped and took me to task. In a gentle, but firm, voice she said, "I may be old, I may be blind but I do not totter. When I go for a walk I like to walk". I got the message and that was the first of many enjoyable outings. Weather permitting, we set off every day. Bella only accompanied us if we were not going too far. She was just middle-aged, of perfect sight but without doubt she tottered!

We kept mainly to the roads because it was very wet underfoot and tarmac was easier for Miss Little to walk on. Nonetheless I got to see a lot of the surrounding countryside. We often finished our walk by coming home via the main street. This was a bit like a royal progression. Everyone stopped to say "Hello" to Miss Little. If ever she complained

of feeling bored, I took her for a walk up the main street. Although boredom was not something I could complain of. By the time I had given Miss Little her breakfast in bed, walked the pooch, fed the birds on the bird table and cleared the lawn of Bella's ministrations, the morning was well advanced. Then visitors would start popping in and endless cups of coffee would be followed by equally endless glasses of sherry. Miss Little had a very generous nature and did not believe in serving sherry in 'piddling' little glasses but used some Waterford urns. We got through sherry at an alarming rate. The wine merchant in the village probably thought that we were a pair of old soaks. Fortunately, he delivered so I was saved the embarrassment of continuously clanking my way up and down the village. Miss Little's generosity also extended to the electricity, she was always turning lights on. Obviously, they made no difference to her, she did it solely for my benefit.

"It's such a dark cottage, dear, I don't want you sitting in the gloom".

It was wonderful. Alan had forever been turning lights off. His perpetual moan was that our house looked like the Blackpool illuminations. I liked the home to be bright and cheerful and as we weren't exactly existing on Doris's old age pension, rather the mafia millions, we could afford it. Latterly it had become such a bone of contention between us that Alan would go round the house turning off all the lights and I would follow a few minutes later and turn them all on again. Really how trivial could one get. The world was in chaos around us, the country was in recession and Alan and I spent all our energy and thought processes turning lights on and off!

Nonetheless I was concerned about Miss Little's finances and her situation. She may, for all I knew, be a very rich

woman but, if having full-time help was expensive, then having temporary help on a permanent basis was astronomic. The first time I packed up the laundry I realised that it was costing about £12 per week and I also realised that my late mother's frugality was rubbing off on me — I was horrified. Not only that I was completely unable to ignore the situation. A quick calculation showed that capital cost of buying and installing a washing machine would be offset within the year against laundry bills. All my innate bossiness rose to the fore and I broached the possibility of buying a washing machine with Miss Little. It had crossed my mind that Miss Little might dislike washing machines and that it was by preference that she used the laundry. However, she struck me as a very down to earth, sensible sort of person who, notwithstanding her generous nature, would not want to pour money down the drain, which is effectively what she was doing. I was right. Miss Little immediately saw the sense of my idea and apparently had frequently thought about it herself but could not visualise how to fit the item into her tiny kitchen. With a bit of reorganisation, we soon solved that problem and just as we were discussing it a neighbour popped in who recommended an excellent plumber. Quick as a flash I was on the telephone and the very obliging man agreed to come round the next evening to assess the situation and give Miss Little a quote.

Miss Little was absolutely delighted to have someone take the initiative so I decided to strike while the iron was hot and tackle the subject of permanent help. I have never been one to mind my own business and if I went on like this, I would probably get the sack from the agency (I seem to be encouraging all their customers to leave them) but, undeterred

and with my calculator still in my hand, I managed to give her the figures which showed that she was spending at least 30% more money than she needed. Further conversation revealed that if I had no idea how rich Miss Little was, nor did she. Even without the consideration of finance she admitted that she felt she might, on balance, prefer a permanent housekeeper to the constantly changing, albeit sometimes stimulating, temporary help. Her two anxieties were finding a suitable person and the accommodation she had to offer. The latter was easily eliminated. My bedroom was charming and there was a room next door which Miss Little described as the dog room but in reality, was a junk room. Bella slept in Miss Little's bedroom and all the junk could be moved out and stored in the garden shed. The dog room would then make a perfect sitting room, it even had a grate in it. Finding the right person would be more of a poser. Fortunately, I discovered an agency in Oxford which could undertake the task. All applicants were personally vetted, a trial period was guaranteed and the commission was only paid on a satisfactory placement. Miss Little was in a very vulnerable position being both elderly and blind and she was naturally anxious that she might be saddled with someone whom she initially liked, but who turned out to be quite unsuitable. Valid fears, but the agency was a reputable, well established one and the trial period could be up to ten weeks which should be sufficient time to discover the workability of a relationship.

Miss Little was definitely interested but understandably wanted to discuss the matter with her financial advisor from the bank. By sheer good fortune he was coming to see her on my day off so I prepared some facts and figures for her to show him which would enable him to properly consider the

proposition and give her the necessary advice. Apparently, it was he who had advised Miss Little to date to stick to my agency, warning her against the dangers of employing permanently someone about whom they knew nothing. The night before the said man from the bank was due to arrive, I explained to Miss Little that if she employed someone on a permanent basis she would be responsible for administering the PAYE and deducting the National Insurance contributions, but presumably the bank would be able to handle this for her. I wished I hadn't opened my big mouth. Immediately Miss Little went into total panic, it was all beyond her. Nonetheless she is an astute old lady and she could see the merit of my proposition, she just couldn't cope with the logistics, but she could cope with people. With the sweetest smile she said, "My dear you are so clever please will you talk with the man from the bank tomorrow?" Bang went my day off! In fairness I had initiated the whole scheme so perhaps it was only right that I pursued it until it was either adopted or scrapped. I have also come to the conclusion that old ladies can be cunning creatures. The Hon Mrs Westwood and Miss Little, despite coming from the same rung of the social ladder, were seemingly poles apart in personalities but now some remarkable similarities were appearing!

With the arrival of the financial adviser in mind I thought I had better climb out of my jeans and into a skirt so as to look reasonably business-like. I didn't want him to think that I was clueless female unable to think beyond the kitchen sink. The financial adviser turned out to be rather a dish and was undoubtedly impressed with my grasp of facts and figures. I just silently thanked whoever had invented the pocket calculator. He agreed with me that the agency I had discovered

in Oxford would appear to be as safe a way as possible of attempting to find someone suitable and he said that he would ascertain if the bank could handle the administration of the PAYE system and the National Insurance contributions. We had definitely made progress and the subject of the washing machine took all of two seconds to decide. He told me to go out straight away and buy one. As it was a day of torrential rain and early closing in Oxford my enthusiasm had to be curbed for twenty-four hours but I spent a pleasant afternoon measuring up. I didn't want all my wonderful plans to be brought to nought by buying a machine that didn't fit into the rather limited space available. I even measured the narrow doorways. I really would have ended up with egg on my face if the machine fitted beautifully into its appointed slot but couldn't actually get into the cottage in the first place.

With everything firmly under control and feeling very pleased with myself I went for a stroll in the village in the pouring rain. Miss Little declined the offer of a walk, getting soaking wet was not her idea of fun, so as I was on my own, I pottered in and out of the astronomically expensive shops. I finally found a 'nearly new' shop down a little alleyway which had for sale the most gorgeous faux fur-lined raincoat. It was just like the Mondi ones and looked brand new. Temptation got the better of me and I tried it on. It was perfect and it even looked good over wellies. It was big, long, warm and looked truly expensive. The assistant gushed, my feeling of well-being suddenly extended to my purse and I bought it without even the slightest twinge of conscience. It was just as well that the assistant had told me that the faux fur lining could be removed so that it became simply a mac. I was thus able to console myself, when guilt set in on the walk back to the

cottage, that I had really got two coats for the price of one —
a bargain! The fact that what I had spent on it was probably the
same as my gas and electricity bills put together was irrelevant.
If my gas was cut off, I would need such a coat to keep me
warm. It was just as well that the dishy financial advisor did
not have insight into my thought processes when it came to my
own finances!

Miss Little was delighted with my purchase. By this time,
she had winkled out of me all the history that had led up to my
appearing on her doorstep and she thought a little extravagance
was just what I needed to cheer me up. I passed her the coat,
she ran her hands all over it and pronounced it a snip.
Nonetheless as I departed the next day to look for a suitable
washing machine Miss Little laughingly warned me that her
own spirits were already high and an ultra-expensive washing
machine was not required, so would I please curb my
extravagant impulses!

The outskirts of Oxford were a nightmare. There was a
maze of road works, traffic lights and nose to tail traffic none
of which was moving at all. It was hard to tell which roads
were one way and which had two-way traffic. Certainly, the
old lady in the car behind me couldn't tell, but that was
probably because her eyes didn't reach above the steering
wheel. I surmised that she drove by extra-sensory perception
rather than by actually seeing. Anyway, she suddenly overtook
me and shot off down the right-hand side of the road.
Unfortunately, we were not in a one-way street, and after about
one hundred yards she met an extremely large McVities lorry
coming the other way. This created an impasse. Our lane of
traffic was not moving at all and the cars behind me had swiftly
closed up to take the little old lady's place in the queue. The

lorry certainly couldn't back up because he had a line of traffic behind him and nowhere to go. Additionally, until his line of traffic could move it was blocking the road works. Therefore, my line of traffic was unable to move even if the lights did eventually turn in our favour. The little old lady had done a magnificent job of bringing the outskirts of Oxford to a grinding halt. There was only one solution, our heroine had to reverse up the road until she could find a side street and get out of the way. The lorry driver told her this in fairly expletive terms which simply had the effect of reducing the recipient to tears. Nick and Simon always, jokingly, maintain that I was only put on this earth to embarrass them, part with the cash and do the washing! I am rapidly coming to the conclusion that I should add helping little old ladies to this list. This little old lady was clearly incapable of backing her car any distance and everyone was losing their tempers. So there was no alternative, I got out of my car and offered to reverse the offending vehicle out of the way. The poor dear was overwhelmingly grateful but it took some time to extricate her from the driver's seat and into the passenger's seat and then I had to reverse some five hundred yards to the nearest side street. Leaving the old soul incoherent with relief I sprinted the five hundred yards back to my car before I started to hold up the traffic. The McVities' lorry driver did wave at me as I was puffing and panting up the street and he was roaring off down a clear road!

Oxford was also impossible to park in but finally I found a space and located the MEB showroom. January is a good time of year to be buying electrical goods, everything was in the sale and I found a splendid machine for £299. Miss Little was going to be truly pleased with me. The only snag being that if she did decide to go ahead, I was going to have to come

back to Oxford to order it — orders over the telephone were not permitted.

As I had anticipated Miss Little was pleased. She really was becoming very excited at the prospect of owning a washing machine and, yes, she wanted to set the scheme in motion. I rang the obliging plumber, who had already given us an acceptable quote for the installation, and who even more obligingly agreed to do the work a week on Saturday at no extra cost. He worked for himself and apparently had never heard of the dreaded word 'overtime'. I was just keeping my fingers crossed that the quality of his workmanship was up to the quality of his amenability.

The next day was my postponed day off and I had arranged to meet an old school friend, Nina who lived not far away, for lunch in Witney. I braved Oxford first and ordered the washing machine. Lunch was spent first of all sorting out the affairs of the world, concentrating mainly on the Prince and Princess of Wales, Saddam Hussein came a very poor second, and then sorting out the affairs of Hannah. I had taken with me a letter that had arrived from Alan that morning.

The good aspect of being a helper is that you appeared in people's lives as though you had come from another planet. If you wanted, you could be devoid of a past and your only future would be the person you were going to look after next. It was a little bit like living in limbo. Miss Little had been the first person to have really penetrated me and my troubles and she had made me realise that I can't live in this limbo forever. Soon I was going to have to decide whether I go it alone or if a reconciliation, now that I know what the outside world was like, might be possible. Originally when I had packed my bags and left it had been an irrevocable and final decision. I had not

left on an hysterical whim. It was only as a result of Nick and Simon's counsel that I had agreed to take some 'time out' to begin with. The letter from Alan proved to be a request that we visit a counsellor together. That and a glass of wine inspired me to indulge in a splendid morass of guilt, self-pity, despair and self-analysis which was actually quite satisfying but not, as Nina very tartly told me, in the least bit constructive. Her simple but firm advice was, "go with Alan to a counsellor and sooner rather than later".

I returned from my lunch in a very reflective mood and decided that I would agree to meeting Alan with a counsellor at the end of my stint with Miss Little. It was just as well that I had already made that decision because on my return I found that Miss Little, who had also been out to lunch, was suffering from violent indigestion and Bella, probably out of sympathy, had left unpleasant little messages all around the house. It was straight back to work and no time to think of errant husbands and possible reconciliations.

The next few days were spent reorganising the larder to make room for the famous washing machine. I have never known such a simple task take me so long, not because it was onerous, merely because I was constantly interrupted by a stream of visitors that kept popping in — nieces, friends, Miss Little's social worker. I became fairly adept at preparing a tray of coffee with one hand whilst sorting out piles of Pyrex dishes with the other.

Nonetheless I did encounter a small set back to all my plans which dampened my enthusiasm a bit but not for long. The splendid (or so I had thought) agency in Oxford rang to say that, on reflection, finding Miss Little the kind of housekeeper that she required was not really their speciality

and regretfully they would be unable to assist. Oh how are the mighty fallen!

In fact, Miss Little was still undecided whether to remain with temporary help or try to find someone permanent, there were pros and cons to both. However, she agreed with me that it would be sensible to have the groundwork organised so that if, either her money looked like running out or she had a stream of hopeless helpers who drove her to despair, she would be able to put the wheels in motion. Dishy financial adviser reported that the bank would be happy to administer the PAYE and Insurance contributions, for a small charge of course! There just remained the problem of finding a reputable and competent agency. The investment of 60p in a copy of *The Lady* magazine soon supplied the solution. Many agencies specialising in finding housekeepers and companions for the elderly and disabled advertised in this periodical and a few telephone calls resulted in several that would fit the bill. There was nothing further that I could do on that score.

Miss Little was such a sweet soul that she became very concerned that all my efforts on her behalf were preventing me from having sufficient time off. Actually, I was perfectly happy and I didn't particularly want to wander round the enticing shops in case my wayward, shopaholic tendencies came to the fore. I have undoubtedly spent all I can currently afford on my gorgeous mac. I had no great desire to explore the surrounding towns and villages. Just the thought of parking was enough to put me off. Similarly, the inclement weather did not inspire me to set off on long country rambles. Nonetheless in the end, just to appease Miss Little, when a friend called in for tea, I announced that I was going out for the afternoon. I went to the local tea shop and indulged in an enormous, gooey,

delicious Danish pastry. Merely looking at it probably put on two pounds and actually eating it a further two. Just as I was beginning to wonder if I would have to stave off indigestion, I also began to wonder if Miss Little's concern for my absence of leisure might not also coincide with a desire to be able to have an indiscreet chat with her friend. If so, I didn't blame her, it must be so trying always to have a relative stranger within earshot. Miss Little was also hampered by not knowing if her helper was in the room or not. She had confided in me, when we were discussing the subject of permanent help, that she hadn't really liked my predecessor. Under the impression that this helper had left the house for her day off, Miss Little made a few pithy remarks to Ethel who was cleaning. Unfortunately, the helper hadn't departed and was, understandably, most affronted. I was quite happy to suffer some minor indigestion and gain a small amount of weight if it gave Miss Little the opportunity for a thoroughly good gossip!

The washing machine was duly delivered at the appointed hour and fitted neatly into the space that I had created for it. Now all that was required was for it to be plumbed in. I was becoming a mite anxious, everything was going too smoothly and I had this niggling suspicion that catastrophe might be hiding just around the corner.

The day dawned, the plumber arrived punctually and everything went like clockwork. The only drama was when I dropped a pile of china emptying a cupboard. The sole reason for this task was because the piping had to go along the bottom of the cupboard and the plumber was anxious in case the vibration from his drilling caused the china to fall and break. He was between a rock and a hard place — vibration from his

drilling or my clumsiness! Fortunately, the china fell onto a mat and remained intact. I really felt that my reputation was on the line with this whole project and it would have been faintly ridiculous if it was my clumsiness that blew it.

The plumber finished his job and we tested the machine. It filled up and it drained with not a leak in sight. Miss Little was thrilled to bits and with much excitement we put on the first load. I went to bed that night in a positively euphoric mood. Next morning peace reigned and my feeling of well-being continued. Bella and I strolled up the main street, I bought the *Mail on Sunday*, and on our return, I settled down to a happy half hour in the kitchen to read it. I was thoroughly engrossed when a continuous dripping sound penetrated my consciousness. I looked up to see the kitchen floor awash with water and Bella having an idyllic time paddling around in it. Such was the quality of the *Mail* that I hadn't noticed the water swirling around my feet and now I couldn't believe my eyes. A swift investigation showed water dripping rapidly from the drain pipe of the radiator the plumber had had to remove and then replace yesterday. There was no way to stop it but fortunately I could get a bowl under the pipe to catch the drips. A telephone call to the plumber was the next order of priority. Sunday notwithstanding, he was going to have to come out, I couldn't spend the next 24 hours changing bowls every five minutes. Unbelievably the plumber was as obliging as ever and promised to effect repairs within 15 minutes. He really should go in the Guinness Book of Records. Whilst waiting for him to arrive I mopped up the kitchen floor and the whole episode was over before Miss Little surfaced downstairs — thank goodness she was not an early riser. My possibly existent God also received a fervent thank you that the leak (which had

been caused by the nut of the drain being loose) had not developed in the middle of the night. It would have flooded the whole ground floor of the cottage.

My relief was short lived. In all the excitement last night I had forgotten to put any milk in Miss Little's jug on her early morning tea tray. She made her own tea in her bedroom in the morning and spent a pleasant half an hour or so sipping it. This morning, when Miss Little realised that she hadn't got any milk, and not liking to wake me at 6.30 am, she had made her way downstairs to get some. She wouldn't have known if the floor was flooded and might easily have slipped and done herself a serious injury. I went hot and cold and thoroughly shaky just thinking about it. Apart from the fact that I might have killed Miss Little, even if she had only been injured, we would probably have had to cancel the Sunday lunch to which we had been invited by one of her friends and to which she was greatly looking forward. Miss Little thought the whole incident was splendidly hilarious when I told her what had happened. She gave me a big hug and told me to stop worrying as I was the best thing that had happened to her in a long time — she definitely had a very generous nature.

Sunday lunch proved to be totally diverting and completely took my mind off washing machines and associated dramas. Our hostess was delightful and we had a delicious meal but by far the best bit was her tale of how they had sold their big house when they moved to their current cottage. Apparently, an uncouth man had appeared unannounced on their door step with his back pocket full of £100 notes and stated categorically that he wanted to buy their house no matter what the price. Mrs Kershaw promptly told her husband that the man must be a train robber and to have

nothing to do with him. Well, they do say "money talks" and few can resist getting the price they want. Understandably the Kershaws duly sold their house to the owner of all that cash. However, according to the local police constable this man, gentleman was hardly the way to describe him, really was thought to be one of the Great Train Robbers. Apparently, he was alleged to have driven the getaway car. Unfortunately, there hadn't been sufficient evidence so no arrest could be made but the amiable PC was determined to arrest him for some offence and have him behind bars before he retired from the police force. Every week the PC would call to visit Mrs Kershaw for a cup of coffee and a chat and he was a great talker. He also had an extremely ill-fitting set of false teeth so when he arrived, he would solemnly take out his teeth and place them on the dresser in order to be able to hold forth more easily. The day of his retirement finally dawned and he appeared at the Kershaw's cottage flushed with excitement. The false teeth were extracted with a triumphant flourish and he proudly announced, "I've done it!" The PC and his fellow constables had eventually managed to arrest the Great Train Robber for receiving stolen goods, namely thousands of cigarettes that had fallen off the back of a lorry. Chicken feed compared to his previous heist but sufficient for him to get his just desserts.

The Great Train Robber then, apparently, sold the Kershaw's former home to another villain who took out all the hedges and was reputed to deal in contraband. It was amazing what went on in sleepy country villages.

My time with Miss Little culminated, predictably, in a farewell meal given by some neighbours. My life at the moment seemed to consist of a series of nervous first days and

festive last nights, or last lunch on this occasion, and marvellous neighbours were undoubtedly an integral part.

I knew it would be a sad goodbye the next morning as I had grown very fond of Miss Little but I hadn't expected it to be quite so heart-warming. She took both my hands and said, "part of me wants very much that you will come for another stint as my helper, when permitted by the agency, the other part hopes that you won't because you can't, the reason being that you have resolved your issues and found a fulfilling way forward — one that makes use of your many talents." I left with tears in my eyes.

# CHAPTER SIX

True to my promise I arranged to meet Alan at a counsellor's house to see if we could find a way forward. I did wonder later if I went with a truly open mind but, at the time, I had hoped that maybe Alan would actually try to understand me and that maybe a reconciliation could be possible. It was not to be. At £25 per hour the counsellor told me that I was very verbal and not much else. Well, I could have told her that for nothing and, in any case, surely the whole point of going to a counsellor was for us (which included me) to talk and bare our souls. She did nothing to assist me or advise how I might cope with life differently or suggest to Alan how he might do things differently. Instead, she listened patiently to Alan, who droned on about how he couldn't understand what had made me walk away from the perfect life that he had provided, and quite simply she lapped it up. She looked at me as though I must be deranged and clearly thought that Alan was now faced with insuperable problems. She was right he did have problems now. He was minus a wife, housekeeper, painter/decorator and secretary and his ego had taken a massive blow but these problems need not have been insuperable with a bit of give and take. I came away from the session feeling that a reconciliation would never be possible, perhaps because I was as incapable of giving and taking as Alan.

So now, in a somewhat depressed state of mind, I had arrived back in Surrey, and if I had hoped for another Miss

Little, I was sadly disappointed. For my sins I have ended up as a helper to a male chauvinist. I have left the serenity and happiness of Miss Little's ordered world and been plunged into the chaos of a large, untidy, cluttered house owned and lived in by a 55-year-old bachelor. The paucity of information supplied by the agency hadn't prepared me and within five minutes of arriving I was heartily glad that my stay was for two weeks only.

The engagement was another last minute one. I had been hoping for a few days of peace and quiet in Wales to recover from my futile counselling session with Alan. However, Mr Keith Sinclair had abruptly found himself bereft of his housekeeper and was incapable of coping on his own. Help was required immediately. Having had such success with Miss Little I was full to the brim with a crusading spirit and I was quite sure that no-one was more capable of coping with this bereft bachelor than myself and it would have the added bonus of taking me out of my depressive state. With my newly acquired experience of employment agencies, I would soon find him a replacement housekeeper and in the meantime, Mr Sinclair would have the benefit of my ministrations.

Mr Sinclair proves to be a large, florid man with an abrupt, discourteous manner. He certainly had no intention of letting me forget that I was merely the hired help. He was extremely irritated that my time of arrival had meant that he had missed a goodly portion of his working day. I had no sooner driven into the very attractive courtyard than I was shovelled out of the car, given a long appraising look (at the moment I was quite relieved to look a bit 'granny like' as I certainly didn't want Mr Sinclair to be tiptoeing around the house at night) escorted into the house, shown the kitchen, my bedroom and given my

marching orders. They were very precise — clear up the mess and make sure there was a decent dinner ready for him at 7.30 pm and off went the charming man who was to be my 'boss' for the next two weeks. He didn't even pause long enough to explain why his housekeeper and upped and left so suddenly. She probably couldn't take another minute of the servitude expected of her and had wisely decided to cut her losses.

One of my flatmates and friend from secretarial college had gone, as her very first job, to a solicitor's office in the City. This solicitor had been bereft of a secretary for several days. As soon as Caroline had taken off her coat the solicitor had sat her down and dictated solidly all day, with hardly a pause for lunch. At the end of the day Caroline smiled sweetly, put on her coat and never went back. She and I spent the evening in the local wine bar trying to decipher the gibberish in Caroline's pad. She had never been very adept at shorthand and all the legal terminology had been beyond her. A bottle of wine later we decided that it was a hopeless task and that the only solution was to jump ship. I now felt like heeding my own advice and following suit. In the end I felt that such a course of action, at my advanced years, was a bit spineless so I just got on with the job.

Having dumped my bag, I decided my first task was to investigate what the kitchen had in the way of food if I was to have a decent dinner on the table at 7.30 pm. The mess would have to wait. The kitchen was a sizable room and was equipped with every latest appliance, including a microwave oven which I hadn't got a clue how to operate, but in an indescribable state. Mr Sinclair was right, he had no idea how to look after himself. How on earth he had ever managed to reach the ripe old age of 55 was a miracle. I could only imagine that originally there

had been a doting mother in his life before the advent of a housekeeper.

The larder revealed a mouldy loaf of bread and a few nondescript cans of soup and vegetables. The fridge contained half a bottle of milk, some stale cheddar and a tub of margarine. Hardly the ingredients with which to prepare a feast. There was nothing for it but to do some rapid thinking, make a quick list and head for the nearest supermarket. Having so recently been with the Chadwicks I had got to know this part of Surrey quite well and therefore knew exactly how to get to the nearest Sainsbury (which hadn't existed when I lived in Surrey as a child). What I didn't know was what Mr Sinclair envisaged when he glibly talked about a decent dinner. I knew that he needed a crash course at the local charm school, but did he want a three-course dinner or what? The other minor concern was that he had failed to give me any housekeeping money. Such a trivial matter for the male mind but I actually wouldn't be able to get out of Sainsbury without any. Fortunately, I had got my cheque book and cheque card!

Since I had no idea as to Mr Sinclair's likes or dislikes, whatever I chose was going to be a gamble. Additionally, I hadn't had time to ascertain the extent of his pots and pans but judging by the excellence of the electrical appliances presumably he had plenty, they just might not be clean. I settled for egg mousse topped with caviar (lumpfish roe really but caviar sounds better) as a starter, followed by boeuf bourguignon with potatoes dauphinoise and a green salad and rounded off with oranges in brandy. If by a decent dinner, he meant fish and chips then we were going to be more poles apart than I had originally thought. I also bought some basics, breakfast foods and a variety of cheeses.

I rushed back to Grange House, had a snack lunch and drew breath. A survey of my surroundings revealed a spacious and beautiful period house full of antiques (not surprising as mein host was an antiques dealer) but with unbelievably shabby and tasteless carpets and curtains. The drawing room obviously doubled as an office. The huge kneehole desk in the bay window overlooking a neglected garden was overflowing with papers and what looked like bills. Files were piled up on the floor and bundles of magazines were strewn everywhere. There was a splendid open fireplace which looked cold and cheerless. The ashes looked as though they hadn't been cleaned out this century and the log basket was empty. The dining room was relatively tidy but the dust on the magnificent table was an inch thick. The cloakroom was a nightmare from which I took a hasty departure but my bedroom was lovely and overlooked the garden. It too was dusty and cobwebby and the bed contained a pile of badly folded blankets with not a sheet in sight. Ever mindful of my night's sleep I set about locating the linen cupboard and found a splendid one on the landing. It was choc-a-bloc with linen sheets and pillowcases and vast towels. Someone, somewhere along the line, had been a good housekeeper — probably doting Mama. I made up my bed, flicked off the worst of the dust and repaired to the kitchen.

I was quite sure that Mr Sinclair had never heard of the term 'washing-up'. Since his housekeeper had upped and left, he had quite obviously gone through every pot and pan, cup and saucer, knife and fork in this extremely well-equipped kitchen. The dishwasher was empty so I loaded it and put it on. I then tackled the remainder in the sink. An hour and horribly wrinkly, red hands later there were at least some clear work surfaces. A cup of coffee revived me sufficiently to start

making the egg mousse, which needed time to set, prepare the oranges and start on the main course.

I then felt in need of a breath of fresh air so I went for a stroll in the garden. All my gardening instincts leapt up in revolt, what a waste. So many people can only strive for small, boringly rectangular gardens on which they pour hours of love, time and money. Mr Sinclair, on the other hand, had a wonderful, big, informal garden with a lawn that rolled down to a stream at the bottom, edged with magnificent weeping willow trees. However, the grass was rank and long, leaves lay in rotting masses, overgrown shrubs were entangled with each other in a death wish confusion and the whole scene was one of melancholy. I itched to find some gardening tools and get started, but that was not my brief. I was here to produce some reasonable meals and restore the house to order. On the way back indoors, I noticed a pile of logs and decided to collect some so that I could light a fire in the drawing room. Perhaps a cheerful blaze in the hearth might warm up Mr Sinclair's cold persona. The logs were under a ramshackle corrugated iron roof and so were quite dry. All I needed now was some kindling. One of the buildings surrounding the courtyard revealed some wooden crates, ideal for kindling. Considerably heartened I went in, cleared out the grate, laid the fire and filled the log basket. As time was getting on, I thought I had better check on dinner and lay the table in the dining room.

At this point I was faced with a dilemma — did Mr Sinclair like to eat his decent dinner in peaceful solitude, or was I expected to join him. I wasn't quite sure of my position and was in a quandary. Up to now I had always eaten my meals with my charges, but then they had all been charming people and I had been there not only to help but also to be a

companion. I had no particular wish to be Mr Sinclair's companion and he clearly did not want me to be one. So did I bob in and out of the dining room serving dinner, like Doris's mother the parlour maid, or did I lay myself a place at the feast? Well, I certainly wasn't put on this world to be a parlour maid, a demeaning helper perhaps but not a parlour maid. Nor was I put on this world to be where I was not wanted, so I laid a single place at the end of the table. Mr Sinclair could enjoy the fruits of my culinary skills in solitary splendour,

At 7.00 pm I lit the fire in the drawing room with the hope that it would be burning brightly by 7.30 pm. It was probably inevitable that all didn't go according to plan. Instead of burning brightly the fire belched out smoke like one of Ted's steam engines. I should have realised that a fire had not been lit in ages, that the chimney was most probably damp and needed sweeping, or worse still was full of birds' nests in which case my next task would have been to call the fire brigade.

Frantically I opened the bay window and left the door open to create a through draught. Then with streaming eyes I rushed into the kitchen to turn down the boeuf bourguignon, which I could hear and smell boiling over on the hob, but which should have been simmering gently. I madly opened all the downstairs windows because the smell of smoke and burnt food was filling the house. I was looking decidedly fraught and it was 7.30 pm. I expected Mr Sinclair to burst in through the smoke like the genii of the lamp but my luck held. As a result of his delayed start to the day he had similarly had a delayed end to it. Mr Sinclair strolled in at approximately 7.55 pm to a welcoming fire in the drawing room and his dinner ready. If he thought that the house was unexpectedly chilly, he had a very

efficient central heating system I later discovered, he made no comment and I didn't enlighten him about the dramas. Mr Sinclair remained in blissful ignorance of the fact that he might have returned home to a somewhat larger conflagration and the courtyard full of fire engines. It would, at least, have solved the problem of the mess!

I had made the right decision with regard to table laying. A brief, "Good evening" was followed by my orders. "Give me five minutes to wash and grab a whisky and then serve dinner".

No please, no thank you and not even the glimmer of a smile. I was not just angry, I was also completely nonplussed. I was simply not used to this reaction from people. One of the reasons I had opted for being a helper, apart from the obvious one that I was not qualified to do much else and I certainly wouldn't be able to remember how to do shorthand, was because I enjoy the company of the human race and I have never previously encountered any problems getting on with diverse personalities. I wasn't sure that Mr Sinclair had even noticed that I was actually a human being. Maybe he thought he was getting a robot from the agency. I had even made an effort and put on a skirt — all the better for me to bob a curtsey in apparently!

Dinner went without a hitch and also without conversation. No suggestion of "that was delicious" or even "that was unacceptable please do not serve it again". By the time it came to coffee I decided that I had had enough. Apart from anything else Mr Sinclair owed me money for my shopping trip to Sainsbury but I also needed to know a little bit more about the domestic arrangements and was he planning to replace his housekeeper and if so, how? As I put the coffee

on the table, I took a deep breath, pulled out a chair and sat down. Well at least I had finally elicited a reaction — surprise! To be fair, once tackled Mr Sinclair proved to be perfectly reasonable. He apologised for not giving me any money, with the rush that morning he had never given it a thought. He pulled out his wallet and handed me £200. Apparently, dinner had been perfect, he had no particular likes or dislikes but preferred variety. Finally, the finding of a new housekeeper was to be left to me. I was to draw up a shortlist of suitable applicants and he would interview them in the evenings. Mr Sinclair made it clear that he didn't want to be bothered with trivia. He merely required his help to provide breakfast and dinner and keep the house in order. Currently I had my doubts as to whether I would be able to find even one suitable applicant. What should I tell any employment agency, "required a super-efficient lady with a skin like a rhinoceros and the ability to keep silent at all times". I had had enough for one day, that problem could be held over until tomorrow.

I cleared up the dinner dishes and retired to my bedroom. As I sat on the bed it suddenly occurred to me that somewhere in the house lurked the used sheets that had come off this piece of furniture and probably piles of other washing as well. I felt certain that the housekeeper when making such a hasty retreat wouldn't have bothered to do the laundry before she shook the dust of Grange House from her shoes. There wasn't a washing machine in the kitchen so there must be a utility room somewhere because a washing machine was on the pro forma I had received from the agency. I hadn't got any more energy, it was another problem that would have to wait for the morning. I took a sleeping pill, had a bath (fortunately there were two bathrooms so I had one to myself) and went to bed.

Thank goodness for modern medicine. I slept like a log and woke in the morning feeling much more hopeful of being able to get through the next two weeks, although I was developing grave doubts about my ability to remain as a helper for the next twenty years. I thought I might look for something a little less taxing on the nerves for my declining years, but what still remained the problem. Downstairs I put the coffee on, cooked bacon and eggs and laid the table. Mr Sinclair appeared promptly at 8.00 am, grunted "Good morning", ate my offerings whilst reading *The Times* and then departed. You would have thought that someone who was in the buying and selling business might have developed a more approachable manner.

First job on the agenda after breakfast was to find the washing machine. Exploration revealed a door at the end of the walk-in larder which gave onto the utility room containing sink, washing machine, tumble dryer and ironing board. Grange House was a curious mixture of tatty mess and no expense spared. The furniture was all superb and there appeared to be every labour-saving device imaginable. Needless to say, the utility room also contained a large pile of washing — sheets, towels and a vast quantity of shirts. I really disliked ironing shirts. I put on the first load of washing and then retreated back to the kitchen for a cup of coffee and the making of an extensive shopping list. Coffee was an essential ingredient without which I cannot survive. I'm not an alcohol or nicotine addict but caffeine I must have. I found a pad and drew up a menu for the week which helped with the shopping list. I had to admit to myself that I preferred this type of catering to existing on an old age pension. The difference, however, was that Doris unfailingly appreciated the meals that

I served her, whilst with Mr Sinclair I felt I should be lucky if I received anything more than a grunt.

While I was sitting there a little old lady came bustling in and gave me the fright of my life. She really did appear like the genii of the lamp. Maggie, it transpired, cleaned Grange House. Maggie had always cleaned Grange House and Maggie was about 100 years old! She reminded me a little bit of Doris's friend, Dulcie. Unfortunately, Maggie had been ill for the last three weeks, which explained why the house was dusty and dirty, and she was just as surprised to see me as I was to see her. Mr Sinclair hadn't thought to inform her of the housekeeper's abrupt departure, nor the arrival of a temporary helper, any more than he thought it necessary to explain to me that he employed help with the cleaning. Nonetheless my relief was heartfelt, with Maggie's presence I could delegate the worst of the cleaning tasks. Delegating was something I was perfectly comfortable with and with luck ironing shirts might be her forte. I began to feel positively euphoric when I discovered that Maggie came every morning for two hours, Monday to Friday. We would soon have the house looking ship shape.

Maggie was a dollar a minute. She was a Brummie by birth but had married a local man and had lived in Milford ever since. She could never quite remember how many children she had had, it varied from 10 to 12. I'm quite sure that if I had had to produce that many, I would have lost count as well! Actually, I think what caused her confusion was that her last pregnancy produced twins who sadly died at birth. Many of her children had predeceased Maggie and her husband had long since curled up his toes, but she had numerous grandchildren and countless great grandchildren. Maggie was

also a tireless worker and a mine of information. I didn't think it would be long before I knew rather more about the uncommunicative Mr Sinclair.

However, currently there was no more time for chatting. Maggie and I decided on the order of priority for her cleaning tasks and I repaired to the telephone and the yellow pages. I identified several local agencies and contacted all of them. I explained in some depth what was required but I played down what I considered to be Mr Sinclair's less than attractive qualities. I didn't want a repeat of my experience with Miss Little and a negative response after a period of reflection. There was nothing vulnerable about his position and any housekeeper always had the option of voting with her feet if the position didn't work out, as the last one had done. Two agencies believed that they could help and agreed to get back to me as soon as they had anyone suitable. Interviews in the evening did not seem to present a problem. I didn't bother to mention minor details such as shortlists. Time enough to discuss that if it was found that the market was flooded with potentially suitable applicants.

Feeling moderately pleased with myself, I left Maggie waving a duster industriously whilst singing merrily songs from the *'Pirates of Penzance'*, quite tonelessly, and set off for a serious shop in Sainsbury.

Maggie had left by the time that I returned but she had already made considerable inroads in the chaos and Grange House was taking on an infinitely more cheerful air. I had bought some flowers in Sainsbury and having arranged two vases, one for the drawing room and one for the hall, the place began to feel positively like home. The day continued serenely enough, if boringly. I hung out one load of washing, put on the

next, changed the sheets on Mr Sinclair's bed — his bedroom was predictably severely masculine with heavy mahogany furniture and curiously no photographs — prepared dinner and drank a lot of coffee.

Mr Sinclair returned home at the appointed hour and I at least received a polite "Good evening". However, he then went on to drink his whisky, eat his dinner, and finish his coffee without another syllable passing his lips. Charles Forrester may have described himself as a poor conversationalist but I would have described Keith Sinclair as being in training for a Trappist monk. I eagerly looked forward to Maggie's arrival the next morning so that I could discover a bit more about this taciturn gentleman.

Maggie certainly did not disappoint! I decided that the cleaning could wait for half an hour, I made some coffee and we sat down, me in silence and Maggie in full flow.

Grange House had originally belonged to Mr Sinclair's parents and he and his brother, Francis, had been brought up there. Francis had been the elder brother and apparently the star. One of those rather annoying people who are good at everything — brainy, sporty, musical, charming and handsome of course. Additionally, he was the apple of his parents' eyes. In comparison my temporary boss was overweight, spotty, unathletic, dim and poor company. I began to feel quite sorry for him. The parents had been committed Methodists and very strict with the upbringing of their sons. They were also teetotal, never a drop of drink in their house. I was relieved that I never had to make their acquaintance.

Maggie hadn't enjoyed working for Mrs Sinclair very much but she was glad of the job. With all those children to feed she needed the money — I never discovered what

Maggie's husband had done for a living. As I had already surmised Mama had been a superb housekeeper and everything was meticulously kept. However, she had no artistic talent or flair and the tasteless choice of carpets and curtains were hers. Most of the beautiful furniture had appeared since Mr Sinclair had started his career as an antiques dealer.

Francis had, apparently, swanned into Oxford and naturally emerged three years later with a First. Much to everyone's surprise his younger brother also made it to Oxford where he disgraced himself within the first week. Having been brought up in a teetotal household he was completely unaccustomed to alcohol. The temptations of university life were too much, he succumbed and was dead drunk for a week. Despite such an inauspicious start Keith also achieved a First. The Sinclair parents must have been very proud of their offspring.

Sadly, after that, the tale deteriorated. Keith fell in love, got engaged and brought his fiancée home to Grange House to meet the family. Francis' handsomeness and charm proved too much for the poor girl. She felt out of love with Keith and in love with Francis and they were the ones to get married. Keith was inconsolable and the happy couple tactfully went to live in the USA where, naturally, Francis went on to make millions. The parents were tragically killed in a car accident shortly after the wedding and Keith Sinclair had lived on his own in Grange House ever since, a successful antiques dealer but a confirmed misogynist. Frankly, I didn't blame him. Perhaps a motherly type was what he needed for a housekeeper. He certainly didn't need an inveterate talker. Anyway, everything depended on what applicants the two agencies were able to generate.

Having enjoyed our tête à tête Maggie got on with her chores and I got on with mine. We had had no trouble in developing an excellent working relationship.

Just when I was beginning to think that maybe this wasn't such a bad job after all disaster struck. We experienced an extremely cold spell of weather with very heavy frosts which didn't clear all day. Mr Sinclair's central heating system was working well so it never occurred to me that any pipes might get frozen. Mr Sinclair's mind was, of course, way above such mundane matters. It was only when I noticed that it appeared to be raining on a rather splendid tallboy in the morning room, which was at the end of the house and was never used, that I began to smell a rat.

It is amazing how calmly one could look at a catastrophe before panicking but by then I was becoming accustomed to cataclysmic events involving water and flooding. In fact, it was sheer chance that had brought me into the room in the first place. I had been looking for a book to read and the morning room housed quite an extensive library. Initially my feet remained glued to the floor whilst, like a zombie, I failed to believe that this could be happening to me again. Then realisation dawned and I rushed over to drag the very valuable piece of furniture out of the way of the falling water. I rushed into the kitchen and grabbed some towels to wipe the top of the tallboy, Mr Sinclair would be distinctly upset if one of his precious antiques suffered water marks, and then flew upstairs to see where the leak was coming from. The room directly above the morning room was a spare bedroom and I discovered that the leak was coming from a pipe leading to the radiator under the window. Apparently, the cold weather had been too much even for the efficient central heating system.

This end of the house was never used and thus the pipe had frozen without anyone noticing, cracked and with slightly warmer weather had thawed producing a steady flow of brackish water. There was worse to come. The burst pipe ran along the floor and so there was no way that I could get a bowl, or anything else, under it to catch the water — a nightmare. It was also difficult to decide what to do first. Finally, I ransacked the linen cupboard for all those huge towels, some of which I laid on the carpet to absorb the worst of the water. I was anxious that the ceiling of the morning room would descend earthwards. Next, I switched off the central heating, but even without the pump water would continue to leak until the system had drained. It took me some time to locate the mains stopcock but eventually I found it in the utility room and I turned off the water. Next job, yellow pages to find a plumber. Oh, if only Burford was a bit nearer, I could have sent an SOS to the wonderful plumber there. I didn't know where to start. In the end I hit on the idea of calling Maggie. Fortunately, she was in and said she would get hold of her plumber and then come round straight away to help.

Snatching up the laundry basket, I shot upstairs again and changed all the sodden towels for a fresh supply, at the same time mentally blessing Mr Sinclair's Mama for her meticulous and excellent housewifery, there must have been enough towels to supply a hospital. Back down the stairs I went, into the utility room, towels into the washing machine on spin cycle, into the kitchen made myself a very strong cup of coffee and drew breath. My respite was short lived. Time and tide and leaking pipes wait for no man! Back upstairs I went, removed the sodden towels and laid down fresh ones. Then downstairs again with the sodden towels, then back upstairs again — it

was like a treadmill, a very exhausting treadmill. How much water could there be in a central heating system?

Even the state-of-the-art washing machine began to suffer from exhaustion, certainly each spin cycle seemed to take longer. I was now arriving downstairs with the next load before it had finished the previous one. Feeling shattered with the umpteenth pile of sodden towels in my arms dripping everywhere, weighing what seemed like a ton, and nowhere to put them decided me that I had, quite definitely, had enough. I marched to the back door and hurled the laundry basket, with its load of sodden towels, as hard as I could into the wide blue yonder accompanied by a string of truly bad language. The basket landed at the feet of an extremely startled plumber. I had the grace to blush and Maggie roared with laughter. The plumber must have thought that he was seeing an apparition. Apart from my extensive, unrepeatable vocabulary I was wild-eyed, wild-haired and, despite the freezing conditions, in bare feet. I had taken off my shoes and socks all the better to paddle in the puddle in the bedroom.

Maggie and I repaired to the kitchen to make some more coffee whilst leaving the plumber to work miracles upstairs. This didn't take as long as it might because, although he had to drain the system to repair the leak, I had been very effectively doing that job for him for what had seemed like an eternity. Refreshed by the coffee Maggie and I went to view the damage in the morning room. The tall boy was fine. The carpet was a bit damp, so we washed it in case the radiator water would leave a stain, and the ceiling was intact. There would, undoubtedly, be a water mark but a coat of paint when it had dried would soon solve that problem. Upstairs the carpet was completely waterlogged but only in the area around the

radiator. My operations with the towels had been remarkably effective. Maggie and I decided that it would be pointless to attempt to wash it until the pile had dried out considerably. It only remained for me to take the last of the towels down to the utility room and start the task of washing and drying them all. Actually, that was not all that remained. I still had to explain to Mr Sinclair what had happened. Along with attempted arson I could now add a tendency to create floods to my CV.

Thank goodness Maggie was with me, without her I would have worked myself into near hysteria. However, she matter-of-factly pointed out that Grange House belonged to Mr Sinclair and it was his responsibility to see that it was properly maintained. She also reminded me of my initial orders from him and they hadn't included any reference to being a maintenance engineer. Maggie really was a gem! Nonetheless I had to have two very large whiskies to bolster my courage before Mr Sinclair arrived home.

Mr Sinclair may have been all the things that I have described but as I have previously discovered he was not unreasonable. He took my tale of woe very calmly, complimented me on my initiative and offered me a permanent job. You could have knocked me down with a feather, I was struck dumb. My speechlessness was too much for Mr Sinclair and he burst out laughing. I had never even seen him smile let alone laugh and it completely changed him, he was really quite an attractive man. Even so I didn't want to be his housekeeper. Tactfully I explained that I wasn't in the market for a full-time job just yet but that I greatly appreciated his offer. I added that hopefully I would have a few suitable candidates for him to interview soon. Both agencies were going to get a telephone call in the morning. I had no intention of extending my stay

beyond two weeks but in view of the emergence of a nicer side to Mr Sinclair's nature the least I could do was to make certain this his future comfort was ensured. At least I would now be able to reassure all applicants that their prospective boss's crusty exterior hid not just a heart of unadulterated dross, a little gold lurked there as well. It still needed polishing but there were signs of hope.

Conversation with both agencies the next day revealed that they each had a suitable applicant to offer. Despite the recent recession it would appear that there not hordes of unemployed beating a path to Mr Sinclair's front door, perhaps his reputation had gone before him. I arranged for each applicant to be interviewed on separate evenings at 7.30 pm. I would somehow have to persuade Mr Sinclair that he not only had to be home promptly but that his dinner would be delayed until after the interviews.

I was not successful. The first evening he arrived back at 7.45 pm looking extremely grumpy. I had a sneaking suspicion that he had done it on purpose and that he disliked the prospect before him. His disinclination to loquaciousness might make an interview an ordeal for him but it would also turn it into a nightmare for the poor interviewee.

The first applicant, Mrs Smith, had duly turned up on the dot of 7.30 pm. She was a pleasant woman in her early fifties and looked the motherly type. I had spent the fifteen-minute wait for Mr Sinclair in getting to know her. There was a faint possibility that Mr Sinclair might actually ask my opinion of the applicants so it would be just as well to have formed one. Mrs Smith was an impecunious widow. Her family were all grown up and she not only needed a job but also a home. Her husband had not been a great provider whilst alive and when

dead had left her destitute. Like myself, she was only qualified to run a home. She sounded competent and I liked her. She also had the virtue of being a keen gardener. It would be nice to think that the beautiful garden might be properly cared for. I tactfully explained about Mr Sinclair's brusque manner and stressed that he did not interfere with the running of the house, a polite way of putting that he cared damn all!

The interview took precisely five minutes. Mrs Smith scuttled out of the house like a scared rabbit. I rushed after her to find out what had happened. Apparently, Mr Sinclair had asked if she could cook, if she could manage a house, why did she need a job and when could she start? All the questions had been delivered in his usual peremptory manner and Mrs Smith had been reduced to monosyllabic replies. Mr Sinclair really was his own worst enemy. I managed to cheer Mrs Smith up and she was so desperate that she agreed to take the job if properly offered it. The devil she currently knew was definitely not better than the one she didn't. At Grange House she would be fed, housed, warm and paid and quite honestly contact with Mr Sinclair was so small that it can be survived. In any case I still nurtured the hope that he was not actually as charmless and difficult as he initially seemed.

The second applicant was definitely a match for Mr Sinclair. Miss Hamilton was a wiry spinster, again probably in her early fifties, with a chip on her shoulder the size of a house. I only had a couple of minutes with her first, because Mr Sinclair returned home reasonably promptly, but even then, I didn't get a word in edgeways. Garrulous was a fair description of Miss Hamilton and the interview lasted half an hour. Miss Hamilton left still talking nineteen to the dozen and Mr Sinclair looked punch drunk!

Without waiting for an invitation, I went into the drawing room and sat down in case my assistance was required. Mr Sinclair smiled, he ought to do that more often it suited him, and said, "Mrs Mills compared with that woman you are like the Archangel Gabriel". I quietly preened myself and forbore from reminding him that said Angel was a man. Quite clearly Miss Hamilton was unsuitable but what about Mrs Smith. Alternatively did Mr Sinclair want to wait and see if the agencies could produce any further suitable candidates for the job? Fortunately, Mr Sinclair had had enough of his domestic problems and, realising that my departure was fairly imminent, he decided to settle for Mrs Smith. Since the agency concerned had already taken up her references, which were satisfactory, I was detailed to engage her, sort out starting dates and show her the ropes. I just hoped that my powers of persuasion, coupled with Mrs Smith's very straitened circumstances, were sufficient to inspire her to accept. A short homily to Mr Sinclair on how to treat his housekeeper and thus retain her services would not have gone amiss, but even I quailed at such impertinence.

After dinner I rang Mrs Smith and offered her the job which she accepted without hesitation. On reflection she was quite looking forward to it. Grange House was attractive and commodious so she certainly did not need to be under Mr Sinclair's feet. She had friends and family in the area and the work really was not too onerous now that Maggie was back and the house was in apple pie order. The garden would provide her with a welcome hobby. All in all, the arrangement seemed perfectly satisfactory. Tomorrow I was going to have some time off after all my exertions, so we arranged for Mrs Smith to come round the day after so that she could meet

Maggie and I could give her a lowdown on what was required of her. After an extremely inauspicious beginning this particular assignment had actually turned out to be rather satisfying.

The next day, still flushed with the success of yesterday, I rose, showered, dressed for an outing, made Mr Sinclair his breakfast, greeted Maggie and then left for Guildford. I was in a really buoyant mood and was looking forward to meandering around the shops in Guildford. When I had visited the city with Rosemary Chadwick, we had been so intent on finding her something suitable to wear that I hadn't had time to do any browsing of my own. Today would be different and it was! Once I had pottered up the High Street, I turned into the side street which had housed the art gallery where Michael had worked all those years ago. I was in the mood to go down memory lane and I wanted to see if the place was still there, and it was! It looked just the same and the frontage was still painted an elegant shade of eau de nil. I pushed open the door, the bell tinkled and I walked in. As I walked slowly around the gallery looking at the paintings a voice behind me said, "Good morning, can I help you?"

I would have recognised that voice anywhere, it still had the same wonderfully deep, sexy timbre to it. I turned round to face the man behind and indeed it was Michael. Slightly fuller in the face and with his dark hair now flecked with grey but undoubtedly Michael. He recognised me instantly and immediately enveloped me in an enormous bear hug. It was wonderful — the years just seemed to slip away. Michael was full of questions and wanted to know all about me and I wanted to know all about him. Unfortunately, another customer came in and so we agreed to meet for lunch later on.

For the next two hours I wandered around Guildford in a daze. I simply hadn't expected to see Michael, I had thought he would have moved on many years ago. I wondered about his life, was he married, did he have children, where was he living? All of this I was going to find out shortly.

We met in a small wine bar and ordered drinks and lunch. It was all so splendidly normal and civilised, quite unlike the life I had been leading for the past few months. Ever the gentleman Michael insisted that I start by telling him what had happened in my life since last we met, so I did. It took a long time during which Michael was variously happy for me, sad for me, and sympathetic for me. Just telling him about my recent work with the agency made me realise that I couldn't possibly be a temporary helper for the rest of my working life but my lack of qualifications made finding permanent employment, doing something which had job satisfaction, difficult. Michael fully understood my dilemma but couldn't immediately offer any advice on the matter, but he did say that he would give it thought and knowing him he would.

We had reached coffee before he started to tell me about himself. He had married, not long after I had, someone called Gail who I remembered vaguely. However, she had been on the periphery of our circle of friends so I couldn't recall her in any great detail except that she had been very beautiful. They had bought a house with some land about five miles out of Guildford so that Michael could still keep a horse and Gail had learnt to ride. They had been very happy, although sadly they couldn't have children, and even more sadly Gail had succumbed to cancer five years ago. Michael had bought the art gallery many years ago and had made a success of it ever since. He found finding new artists and displaying their works

enormously satisfying but he also stocked works by better known artists as well, thus maintaining a well-balanced and financially successful gallery. He knew Mr Sinclair and admired his talent as an antiques dealer, definitely more to Mr Sinclair than immediately met the eye, and was amused by my experience of him. Just listening to him talk, his enthusiasm, his infectious grin made it seem as though the intervening 26 years had never happened.

With regret it was time for Michael to go back to the gallery and I had to return to Grange House. I would be leaving Mr Sinclair in two days' time and going straight up to Lincolnshire to look after an elderly widow, thus there could be no possibility of meeting up with Michael again before I left. Fortunately, we both had mobile phones and so we exchanged numbers and promised to stay in touch. I returned to Grange House feeling happier than I had in many months.

I have learnt to enjoy moments of happiness as they occur in the sure knowledge that, currently, they won't last very long. Sure enough I had no sooner got through the front door than my mobile rang, it was Alan. Apparently, he still wanted me to return and even acknowledged that perhaps he could have tried a little harder. I looked at the telephone in complete amazement. Alan had never in all the time I had known him apologised for anything or even admitted that sometimes he might be less than perfect. Once again, if he had just stopped there, I might have been tempted to return. The desperation that had driven me to flee had been completely ousted in the last few months. Now that I knew that I was able to cope with floods, fire and a variety of different personalities and situations, surely living with Alan and the associated problem of coping with the mafia should be much easier. Inevitably

Alan's next sentence quashed all hope of a reconciliation. "You must, of course, by now realise that your behaviour has been completely unacceptable to my family and you will, naturally, give them a full apology for it."

Clearly it was going to have to be onwards and upwards on my own and I told him so.

After a restless, and rather fruitless, night pondering on my future and the next steps to take, it was heartening to see Mrs Smith who arrived with a smile from ear to ear. She had clearly forgotten the brevity of her interview with Mr Sinclair and the fright it had given her. Maggie liked her instantly, which augured well for future relations, and it only remained for me to explain what was required of her.

On Sunday Mr Sinclair enjoyed an avocado mousse, followed by roast lamb and rounded off with chocolate roulade for his lunch. As always, he ate it in solitary splendour in the dining room. Nonetheless he did smile and thank me very much for all my help as I left.

# CHAPTER 7

I was now revelling in the luxury of near stately homes and the incredible hospitality of Lincolnshire. Mrs Davina Thornton is a widow of 83 described as losing her memory, weak on her legs, insistent that she can still drive a car (which she can't) and this can cause problems. It was a source of great mystery to me how the agency managed to concoct these thumbnail sketches, presumably from snippets of information fed back by previous helpers. However, since the situation was usually constantly changing these sketches were invariably only marginally correct.

The drive to Lincolnshire had been tedious and long but uneventful. I had been contacted by Mrs Thornton's daughter, who lived in Suffolk, and she had given me instructions on how to find her mother's house and had agreed to meet me there as the current helper planned to leave at daylight, which struck me as a little unnecessary but perhaps she too had a long journey ahead of her. I knew the feeling. Mrs Thornton's daughter clearly thought that such an early start was not only unnecessary but very thoughtless. It had meant that she, the daughter, had had to make her own long journey from her home in order to be able to give her mother some lunch. I arrived at 2.00 pm and she was gone by 2.15 pm. I thought I spoke quickly but in those fifteen minutes I was shown the house, instructed into the niceties of Mrs Thornton's medications (enough to fill a chemist's shop), given a list of

names and addresses as long as my arm of various friends, informed about the wonderful daily who came every day except Sunday, told me to remember that her mother was to be ready the next day at 11.15 am to do Meals on Wheels (not HAVE meals on wheels but DO meals on wheels) and the daughter then grabbed her car keys and was about to leave. I stopped her. I hadn't yet met Mrs Thornton and I didn't know where to find her. Mother had apparently gone back to bed, where it transpired she spent much of her time.

The house was a wonderful converted mill and as I had driven down the steep drive, I had been greeted by a flock of ducks waddling off to the stream. The beautiful, spacious drawing room was on the first floor and spanned the water. Two huge windows gave a glorious view down the river, the banks of which were covered in aconites and snowdrops. Mrs Thornton's bedroom and bathroom lead off the drawing room and hadn't been pointed out during my whistle stop tour. The daughter halted in her tracks just long enough to introduce me to her mother, whose rather bemused face peeped out from the sheets accompanied by that of a small dog, and then Mrs Thornton's daughter was off. As she left her final words were "Mother hasn't had a bath for ages, she won't have one but don't worry about it". My mind boggled but I was confident that I would be able to persuade Mrs Thornton to have at least one bath whilst I was there, although little warning bells and memories of Mrs Westwood's determination did ring.

This time it really did seem as if my charge was going to prove to be a difficult challenge to look after. At least Doris had got up in the morning and stayed up until I told her it was time to go to bed, even if she spent much of the day dozing in front of the fire. My grandfather, however, always told me

never to be put off by first impressions and he was right.

Mrs Thornton is splendid. She has absolutely no short-term memory. As she succinctly put it, "I don't know my arse from my elbow!" She had obviously been an extremely competent woman and still served a mean gin and French. At about 6 o'clock that first evening she wafted into the kitchen, still in her nightie, and invited me to join her in a cocktail. This proved to be a wine glass full of gin, a whiff of Noilly Prat and a zest of lemon — a real knockout drop. It went straight to my head, which is normally rock-like, and I made a mental note to give that one a miss in the future. Nonetheless our 'happy hour' enabled me to learn that Mrs Thornton had two children, a son and a daughter. They had all lived in the big house at the top of the drive but when Mr Thornton died Mrs Thornton decided that she had eight bedrooms too many and moved into the Mill House, where she has only four. However, she had not completely given into old age and she told me all about her large estate in the Highlands which she has retained and where she gives frequent house parties. Reading between the lines I hazarded a guess that the whole family enjoy this estate and nobly entertain their mother and her guests at given intervals. It must be very distressing for the children to see their mother, who was unquestionably a dominant, no nonsense, capable woman, turn into a lady who asked you the same question ten times in the space of five minutes. I tried very hard always to answer brightly as though it was the first time of hearing. Sometimes I didn't succeed and exasperation entered my voice whereupon Mrs Thornton would apologise profusely for repeating herself. She often said, "what has served me well as a brain all my life serves me no longer". That is the tragedy, she knew that her memory had gone. Her conversation was

perfectly rational and intelligent. She was never confused about her surroundings and to me she was the perfect hostess. I think it was Bette Davis who famously coined the phrase, "old age is not for sissies" and she was right.

I swiftly discovered that Mrs Thornton was possessed of a great many truly good friends. The next morning, I was feeling fairly anxious about the Meals on Wheels business. I had no idea what the form was. Clearly Mrs Thornton was incapable of doing it herself, perhaps I was expected to do it for her, if so where and when? All was resolved. The telephone rang and a Mrs Huntington explained that she and her husband took Mrs Thornton with them to do Meals and Wheels and would I please have her warmly dressed at the top of the drive at 11.15 am and would I later join them for lunch. Mrs Thornton positively leapt out of bed at the mention of her morning's task.

"It's so important to keep up with some of one's charities," she said.

With all this enthusiasm I suggested a bath to which she replied, "of course, dear, I have a bath every morning".

I went into the kitchen feeling fairly smug and was met by the amazing daily. Mrs Taylor is everything she was cracked up to be. A lovely, capable woman who had given years of devoted service to the Thornton family. She had been widowed some years ago and to boost her finances she had done a computer course and now worked in an office in the afternoons. Apparently one of the reasons Mrs Thornton was so fond of Mrs Taylor was because she didn't, "keep her brain in her mop!" It was curiously formal, despite all those years of service Mrs Taylor was still called Mrs Taylor, her Christian name was never used by Mrs Thornton.

We got on well immediately and between us there was no formality. I was swiftly, Hannah, and Mrs Taylor, Mary. Mary was enormously impressed that of her own volition Mrs Thornton was going to have a bath. Unfortunately, it was not to be. At that moment Mrs Thornton came into the kitchen and asked if the Aga was on because the water was only lukewarm. The Aga certainly was on and last night, when cooking dinner, I discovered that it did a marvellous impersonation of a furnace in a forge. It was incredibly hot and the roast chicken and roast potatoes were more like burnt offerings than a tempting meal. However, Mrs Thornton was right, the water was only lukewarm. Mary turned on the immersion but the desire to have a bath had long been forgotten by the time the water had heated up.

Nonetheless Mrs Thornton was dressed and ready in time looking remarkably elegant and in complete possession of her faculties. We walked up to the top of the drive and sat on a convenient bench at the side of the road. We had only been there two minutes when a lady came out of the house opposite with her Labrador dog. She came straight up to us and Mrs Thornton, with a bit of prompting, managed to remember my name and introduced me to the lady, Mrs Foster. Mrs Foster without further ado asked us for drinks that evening and wandered off. The Huntingtons duly arrived in their car and we arranged that I would be in the same place, but in my car, at 12.45 pm and would follow them home.

At 12.45 pm, whilst waiting in my car as directed, a very attractive lady on a horse stopped to ask if I was Mrs Thornton's new helper. It transpired that the lady lived in the big house (Mrs Thornton's old abode) and had been meaning to invite Mrs Thornton for a meal sometime, perhaps Sunday

lunch would be a good idea, she would check with her husband. She should have been quicker off the mark because the Huntingtons forestalled her and we were invited to Foyle Manor for Sunday lunch. I had been in Lincolnshire less than 24 hours and we already had three invitations. So far, I had produced just one meal and that had only been fit for an ancient God. It didn't appear as though I would have to worry too much, in the immediate future, about the convenience of Mrs Thornton's kitchen or the state of her pots and pans which was just as well.

The ground floor of Mill House consisted of a hall, dining room, large kitchen and back kitchen. The large kitchen was furnished more as a breakfast room with a beautiful table, chintz covered armchairs, dresser and chest of drawers but also contained the Aga. The back kitchen had the sink, the working surfaces, the fridge and the larder but no means of cooking. This resulted in an endless rush backwards and forwards whilst cooking and invariably spilling the results on the priceless rugs dotted on top of the tiled floor. The floor was polished to a mirror by Mary and so the rugs skated around in a lethal fashion. If I actually ended up doing much cooking, I was certainly going to have plenty of exercise which had every chance of ending in serious injury. The aids to domesticity came straight out of the Ark. Mrs Thornton possessed the original washing machine, complete with mangle, the original dishwasher and the original Kenwood mixer, none of which I attempted to use. It was amazing that such equipment still existed and that, up until recently, Mrs Thornton had been using it and by all accounts she had been a superb hostess. In fact, I didn't have to prove my skill with the mangle either because Mary was in charge of wash day. In the end I came to

the conclusion that Mrs Thornton's helper needed to be a cross between a chauffeur and a social secretary. Certainly not an onerous job but I definitely had to keep my wits about me.

Mrs Thornton rarely retained any information for more than a few seconds and would accept every invitation with great enthusiasm completely oblivious of any preceding arrangements. I had only reached my second day and already we had conflicting engagements which took some considerable time to sort out because I couldn't be sure if the information Mrs Thornton gave me was actually correct. It would have been so much easier if I could have dealt with all telephone calls and invitations but it was obvious that it was important to Mrs Thornton that she should still control some areas of her life. Tact and diplomacy were clearly much needed skills in this job and not something I have hitherto possessed in abundance. To assist I slowly developed the art of eavesdropping and the information thus gained provided the basis for the subsequent delicate manoeuvring. I found that if I had heard the conversation, or at least one side of it, double booking became less likely.

Mrs Thornton was quite happy to have me around and if I had been out always recognised me and welcomed me home, but she floored one of my friends on the telephone. When my friend rang and politely asked to speak to me, she was met with the response "Do I know her?"

Fortunately, my recent development of large flappy ears and the stoicism of my chum meant that I managed to retrieve the telephone, before she rang off in bewilderment. I had given my friend my mobile number, as well as Mrs Thornton's number, but I rarely turned my mobile on being very unused to the contraption. I made a mental note to keep my mobile

both on and charged.

The weather was, for the most part, glorious whilst I was in Lincolnshire. Bright frosty mornings followed by sunny days. The ducks were a delight. As soon as I pulled back my curtains in the morning they would waddle along and leap up onto the wall outside my window. Approximately twenty of them would line up and jostle each other for the best position for all the world like a crocodile of school children. The ducks were quite obviously waiting for something to eat so in the end I obliged by throwing them bits of bread. It was such a lovely way to wake up. On my days off I explored the countryside and one day I visited Lincoln. The city's cathedral is a beautiful gothic building with stunning views from the roof and the tower and, with my recently found taste for religion, I had a wonderful time exploring it. All in all, I had enjoyed a peaceful, happy day. Unfortunately, the end to my day was neither peaceful nor happy.

Before leaving that morning, I had discussed the matter of locking up with Mary. Mrs Thornton, understandably, didn't like to be locked in but when on her own could take it in to her head to go round locking all the doors. In the end we decided that the best course of action was to leave the front door unlocked and for me to take the keys. Thus, as the front door had a Chubb lock, Mrs Thornton wouldn't be able to lock me out. Excellent idea except that in my excitement to be off on my day out I forgot to pick up the front door keys from the dresser in the kitchen. When I returned, flushed from my day in Lincoln, I found that I was well and truly locked out. I rang the bell but to no avail. Mrs Thornton had clearly retired to the safe haven of her bed whilst on her own and either couldn't hear the bell or was asleep. I felt so stupid! I felt even more

stupid when I realised that I didn't have my mobile phone with me. It was sitting, both on and charged, in my bedroom. In the end I drove round the village until I located a public telephone box. Only then I couldn't remember Mrs Thornton's telephone number. There was no directory in the box but a call to directory enquiries gave me the requisite number. Mrs Thornton answered very quickly and when I explained what had happened her response was immediate, "Of course dearest child I will go and unlock the front door straight away". Mrs Thornton's memory was definitely on hold that day because when I got back to the Mill House the front door was still firmly locked and no sign of Mrs Thornton and no response to the doorbell. Clearly Mrs Thornton had forgotten what she was supposed to be doing. There was nothing for it, I had to go back to the public telephone and repeat the process. It occurred to me that I could spend the rest of the afternoon shuttling backwards and forwards across the village until Mary returned from work and I could borrow her key. Perhaps I sounded faintly desperate the second time I telephoned, whatever Mrs Thornton had the front door open when I drove in and welcomed me with open arms.

I later regaled the tale to Mary who, in turn, regaled the experience of my predecessor. Apparently, they were off on one of Mrs Thornton's luncheon engagements. The helper hadn't envisaged a problem in finding the house because Mrs Thornton told her she knew how to get there and Mrs Thornton is never confused about her surroundings. Ten miles and thirty minutes later they duly turned in at imposing mansion. My predecessor had not previously met their hostess and so, when the front door was opened by a middle-aged lady, she launched into an introduction. The lady looked extremely startled, Mrs

Thornton asked her, "Do I know you?" and the hapless helper realised with embarrassment that they were at the wrong house. It later transpired that their hostess for luncheon had, in fact, lived there but had moved about fifteen years ago when her husband died.

With this story fresh in my mind, I always took the precaution of obtaining instructions before I set off on one of Mrs Thornton's social engagements. Mary was a mine of information but sometimes I had to ring the friends myself. Frequently they said, "Oh don't worry Mrs Thornton will direct you," which made me realise that many of her friends didn't realise how frail she now was. She always sounded so completely on the ball and she was quite open about her loss of memory which made it seem less serious. The wonderful friends didn't realise that in order for me to be able to rely on the directions given by Mrs Thornton I had to be sure that she hadn't forgotten where and to whom she was going!

Mrs Thornton loved gadding about (as she described it) and was always enquiring when her next engagement was. However, I noticed that once out, although she sounded on the ball, she would invariably contribute little to a conversation. Her brave face and intelligence were misleading her friends. Nonetheless I was greatly impressed with their hospitality and their friendship to Mrs Thornton because they undoubtedly didn't invite her for her vivacious company and scintillating conversation. I had a sneaking suspicion the company of a fresh face in the form of the most recent helper was a welcome diversion. A large proportion of Mrs Thornton's friends were widows, like herself, living on their own. Gossip formed a large part of their entertainment and just like Miss Little they were agog to know why I was a helper. Life would have been

so much easier if I could have explained that I had just arrived from Mars. However, in the face of all their generosity and kindness it would have been churlish not to have answered their questions and again, like Miss Little, they were past masters at the art of gentle probing. I met a mixed reaction to my predicament.

All this baring of the soul made me realise that I had to take steps to irrevocably separate from Alan, which meant ultimately a divorce, and find a permanent job. In this resolve I was greatly helped by Michael. One evening he called me on my mobile, I nearly jumped out of my skin when it rang, so little did I use it, and I didn't recognise his number. His voice was even sexier on the telephone and just hearing him made me smile. I made him laugh with all the happenings in Lincolnshire and he was greatly encouraging when I admitted that I needed to re-think my career prospects. He came up with a thought-provoking suggestion — in view of my enthusiasm for cooking and my organisational skills, why didn't I enrol for a catering course with a view to setting up my own catering company. I went to bed that night so happy to have heard from Michael and with my head spinning with the possibilities that he had cast before me.

In the morning I was determined to do some research into catering courses however the busy life at the Mill House prevented me from doing that immediately. There was no handy wine merchant who obligingly delivered so all that gin and Noilly Prat had to be bought and then, of course, there was bath time to tackle. After a near success on my first morning, Mary and I were determined not to be beaten. We decided that a day when Mrs Thornton was going out for lunch would be our best chance. Motivated by enthusiasm for her outing might

get her back in the bathroom. I had left the immersion on permanently because I had no intention of being thwarted once more by tepid water. We decided that if I chivvied Mrs Thornton, which would probably make her obstinate and disinclined to do anything I said, then with luck she might be as good as gold for Mary. Bad cop, good cop ploy. Our plan worked liked a charm. Whilst Mrs Thornton was in the bath, I hastily made her bed so that she would be able to retire back into it if all the effort of bathing proved too much for her. 'More haste, less speed' was amply proved. I was just admiring the immaculately smoothed bedspread when it moved. For a ghastly moment I thought I was hallucinating, then I realised that I must have made the bed with the dog, Flora, still in it. She normally curled up on top of the eiderdown and I had forgotten that first meeting with Mrs Thornton when clearly Flora had been under the sheet as well. I pulled the bedding back and tipped her out. The bed was full of dog hairs and muddy paw marks — quite revolting. There was nothing for it, I got some clean sheets and remade the bed. The condition of her bed may not have worried Mrs Thornton but it certainly worried me and I was at a loss as to how to resolve the matter. Flora was Mrs Thornton's constant companion and she would have been bereft if Flora was not permitted to sleep on her bed. In any case I didn't have the authority to ban her. Any attempt to ensure that Flora's paws were clean when she was in the house was thwarted by the cat flap in the back door. This meant that she could come and go at will. Flora's favourite trick was to go out, leap around in the mud at the side of the stream, bark at the ducks and then rush back to her mistress. In the end Mary and I decided that to change the sheets every day was the only solution.

My reverie regarding dogs and beds was interrupted by a shout for help from Mary. Mrs Thornton, all scrubbed and shiny, couldn't get out of the bath not even with Mary's help. She was like a dead weight. Mrs Thornton didn't have any bath aids to help her out of the bath. She just sat there looking embarrassed and frightened. No wonder she had been loath to have a bath. Fortunately, Mary and I are both fit and strong and we managed to manhandle Mrs Thornton out of the bath. As she sat gasping on the stool she wheezed, "my dears this is so demeaning," and I entirely agreed with her.

It was lucky that I had spent some time with Doris because I knew exactly how to make bath time more pleasurable, a specially designed seat and a non-slip mat would make all the difference. A mat was easy, a visit to Boots would solve that problem but the type of seat required wasn't sold in chemists. I rang the Red Cross first to see if they could help. They couldn't but suggested that I got in touch with Social Services. Mrs Thornton would curl up with embarrassment if she thought that they needed to be involved in her life but there seemed to be no alternative. So I rang Social Services and although the person I spoke to was extremely helpful it appeared that they were unable to supply a seat without a referral. Such a referral would mean that someone would have to come and interview Mrs Thornton and assess her needs. Such is bureaucracy, and what a waste of time and money. All I wanted was a seat for the bath and if I could have managed to buy one in the shops Mrs Thornton was in a position to buy fifty without even batting an eyelid. Nonetheless Social Services were adamant that the correct procedure had to be followed but in view of the fact that I would only be with Mrs Thornton for another week they would try and expedite the

referral. I was not convinced and had visions of months going by before Mrs Thornton had another bath.

I never had any problem with Mrs Thornton and a desire to drive her car. She was always perfectly happy to travel in my car and freely admitted that she no longer drove. It was a chance remark to Mary about this non-existent problem and the inaccuracy of the agency's records that solved the mystery. Apparently one day the gardener had asked Mary if she would just move the car as he wanted to get at some tools at the front of the garage. Once in the car Mary was nearly over-powered by the most appalling smell, something must have died somewhere. She looked all over the place, under the seats, in the glove compartment, down the back of the seats but found nothing. However, when she opened the boot, she was confronted by a bag of shopping containing cream, cheeses, bananas and bacon which had clearly been there for some considerable time. Mrs Thornton must have gone out shopping and then forgotten what she had done. As chance would have it Mrs Thornton appeared just as Mary was about to dispose of the decomposing food. Mrs Thornton realised what must have happened and it shocked her to the core. Although, being the thrifty housekeeper that she was, she did just check to see if anything could be salvaged! The episode had clearly had a salutary effect on Mrs Thornton and, although it would appear that she had originally jibbed at being banned from driving because of her deteriorating health, she now accepted the decision. I made a mental note to correct the agency's records.

Sunday came around as Sunday always does, and naturally, we had to go to church. Mrs Thornton had been the lady of the manor for so long that the duty was ingrained in her. Like me she was not in the least religious (although I am

becoming more open to being convinced in this respect) but, "one has to set an example to the rest of the village doesn't one?" We at least set off in honest frames of mind, Mrs Thornton was doing her duty and I was doing mine. Clearly, however, previous helpers had not been doing theirs. Mrs Thornton's arrival at church was greeted with exclamations of delight. It would appear that the locals hadn't seen her for some time. The sincerity of their welcome was an insight into the great esteem with which Mrs Thornton was held in the village. Nonetheless I discovered that little old ladies were the same the country over, they were a law unto themselves and I have given up blushing. The service was just about to start when the vicar, resplendent in an amazing assortment of robes, started scrabbling about in them, lifting them up and pulling them to one side. Mrs Thornton turned to me and said in what I think was meant to be a confidential whisper, but actually came out in a voice that would have carried across Wembley Stadium "Do you thinking he is looking for a handkerchief or do you think he just wants a jolly good scratch!"

The vicar rushed through that service as though all the fiends in hell were behind him or maybe it was just Mrs Thornton. His sermon was fairly pertinent though. He introduced it with a story about a young man who was signing up to join the Royal Navy. The recruiting officer apparently asked him what his religion was. To which came the answer, "I don't have a religion, I am an atheist". The recruiting officer replied (and the vicar looked Mrs Thornton straight in the eye) "When you are struggling for survival in a life raft, after your ship has been torpedoed and sunk, there are no atheists". He is right, of course, I have sent up many impassioned pleas to the Almighty during the last few months as I have lurched from

one crisis to the next.

Our religious duty done we then departed for Foyle Manor and an extremely pleasant Sunday lunch. After all the 'decent' dinners I had served Mr Sinclair it was a great treat to be wined and dined and in such comfort. The Huntingtons were delightful people and Mrs Huntington had a marvellous sense of humour. Whilst having coffee we looked out of the windows at the sheep grazing on the other side of the ha-ha. One guest commented on the fact that they looked very pregnant and that lambing would probably commence soon. Another guest asked Mr Huntington which vet he had used to perform the artificial insemination. Before Mr Huntington could open his mouth, Mrs Huntington replied, "when we took over Foyle Manor all normal services were resumed. I don't see why sheep should be deprived of their only bit of fun!" Quite a conversation stopper!

On our return to Mill House Mrs Thornton decided that she must give a lunch party to repay all the hospitality we had received. I was in complete agreement. We spent the rest of the afternoon planning who to invite, ten seemed an appropriate number, and what to eat. I have to confess that my spirits quailed a soupçon at the thought of producing an acceptable meal for that many on Mrs Thornton's Aga-cum-furnace. The standard of cuisine that we had been enjoying was exceptionally high, most of the houses we had visited employed staff, but then so did Mrs Thornton — me! However, with the notion that I might enrol for a catering course now firmly planted in my mind, I knew that an ability to be able to rise to the occasion was not just helpful but a necessity.

We finally decided on the guest list, after going through it numerous times, and the menu. There was to be smoked

salmon mousse for the starter, rack of lamb with seasonal vegetables for the main and homemade blackcurrant ice cream and butter tart for puddings. The butter tart was apparently Mrs Thornton's speciality and she was going to give me instructions on how to make it. A short prayer might be in order to assist her in remembering which recipe she was on from start to finish. Otherwise, I might start off making butter tart, and finish making Bakewell tart, the end result probably proving inedible.

Mrs Thornton said that she would telephone everyone in the morning and issue the invitations. However, next morning she was tired after the previous day's frivolities and disinclined to do any telephoning, the invitations would have to wait. In fact, we never did give the lunch party. Mrs Thornton's enthusiasm waned and I hesitated to persuade her or suggest that I issue the invitations on her behalf. An uncooperative Mrs Thornton could spell disaster. A mental picture hovered before my eyes of the guests arriving, the rack of lamb burning to a cinder in the Aga and Mrs Thornton still in bed refusing to get up.

When I discussed the matter with Mary she laughed and then proceeded to tell me the most hair-raising tale which thoroughly convinced me that I had been wise not to pursue the proposed lunch party. Mary had been detailed with the unenviable chore of putting Mrs Thornton on a train from Lincoln at 9.00 am for a visit to her daughter. Even in her prime Mrs Thornton had not been an early riser. The tale went back twelve months to the time when Mrs Thornton was still driving, but even then, her memory was erratic, and for her to rise before 11.00 am, was an unheard of occurrence.

Knowing the problems before her, Mary had rung Mrs

Thornton at 7.00 am to remind her that she must dressed and ready to leave at 7.50 am.

"Of course, Mrs Taylor, I am never late," came the tart reply. Notwithstanding this tartness and assurance, at 7.50 am Mrs Thornton was still wandering around in her lingerie. Mary nearly blew a gasket, persuaded Mrs Thornton into her travelling clothes and fairly bundled her into the car. Mary then set off for Lincoln at high speed desperately trying to ignore the conciliatory comments from Mrs Thornton which threatened to be the last straw.

What Mrs Thornton didn't appreciate was that at 7.00 am, having first telephoned the Mill House, Mary then had to go to the Royal Mail sorting office because the ticket and booked seat slip, which the daughter had posted, had failed to arrive in time. Fortunately, they were in the current batch of post but Mary's normally serene nature had already been severely tested and having to drive like Jehu was not improving the situation. They roared into Lincoln train station with seconds to spare but the saga did not end there.

As she got out of the car Mrs Thornton sweetly asked Mary if she would call in at the kennels on her way back and deliver Flora's blanket which she had forgotten to leave the previous day. Normally Flora travelled everywhere but it was felt that a long train journey, plus an active dog, might prove too much for Mrs Thornton. Despite grinding her teeth Mary apparently managed a strained smile in reply. Fortunately, the kennels were not too much out of her way. Nonetheless when she arrived Mary was confronted by an irate kennel owner who wanted to know where was Mrs Thornton and where was Flora? Mary couldn't understand it. She had been at the Mill House the previous day when Mrs Thornton had set off and

had even drawn her a map so that she would be able to find the place easily. Clearly Mrs Thornton had not arrived but just as clearly Flora was in kennels somewhere. It transpired that there were two other kennels in the vicinity, a small homely one and a large expensive one. Mary tried the small one first but to no avail. However, at the large one she hit the jackpot. There she found an extremely bemused owner and Flora safe and sound. Apparently, Mrs Thornton had swept in yesterday and left her. The owner had tried to explain that the kennels were full and that Flora was not booked in. I could just visualise the splendid Mrs Thornton, as she pulled herself up to her full height, imperiously telling the woman, "of course Flora is booked in, she has been booked in for months, you may take her away," and then sweeping off the premises. Mary apologised profusely and explained the situation. The owner saw the funny side and agreed to keep Flora for the duration. The piece de resistance of the whole comedy was that when Mrs Thornton collected Flora from the very obliging kennels, she commented to Mary that it was "bloody expensive" and vowed that she was never going there again!

Although discretion in respect of the proposed lunch party had undoubtedly been the better part of valour, I did regret that we didn't entertain in some fashion in order to repay all the warmth and kindness that I received during my stay in Lincolnshire. My relationship with Lincolnshire's Social Services was unfortunately not so amiable. Shortly before I was due to leave, I rang to find out what was happening to Mrs Thornton's referral. I spoke to an incredibly snooty individual who said that Social Services had visited Mrs Thornton on a similar mission before Christmas at the request of the District Nurse. On this occasion, inevitably, Mrs Thornton had stated

in forcible terms that she did not require their help, that she was not a cripple and that she had a bath every morning without any trouble. I patiently explained that what Mrs Thornton said, and what was reality, bore no relation to each other. To the snooty individual that was immaterial, if Mrs Thornton said "no" then nothing could be done. I became mildly irritated and went on to point out that Mrs Thornton couldn't remember anything for more than fifteen seconds so little reliance could be placed on her assertions. The answer was still negative. At that stage I became thoroughly annoyed. I was not wanting to commit Mrs Thornton to the local loony bin, I just wanted one bath seat so that she could have a bath. I informed the snooty individual that it had taken two fit, strong women to get Mrs Thornton out of her recent bath. I further informed her that we were not prepared to undertake the task again and therefore Mrs Thornton would have to forgo any further ablutions. That did the trick! Someone from Social Services would visit Mrs Thornton in ten days' time. In fact, that was perfect. It had been arranged that when I left Mrs Thornton would spend the next three weeks visiting her son and daughter. Mary agreed to meet the social worker when she attended the Mill House and with luck the seat would be installed before Mrs Thornton returned. The whole arrangement avoided Mrs Thornton having to cross swords again with Social Services and the indignity (as she saw it) of their involvement in her life.

Mrs Thornton's mind having abandoned the notion of playing hostess digressed to an outing in the country. She had been following with some interest my exploration of Lincolnshire and now she decided that I should visit the coast. A trip to Mablethorpe was needed. It would appear that the

town's great claim to fame was the fact that Mrs Thornton had been born there! The ever-helpful Mary suggested a scenic route and we were ready to set off.

Mrs Thornton was in high spirits and climbed into my car clasping Flora to her bosom. I hadn't anticipated her presence and rushed back into the house to find some rugs to put on the back seat. I didn't want dog hairs all over my upholstery as they were the very devil to remove. I was already going to need a roll of Sellotape and hours of labour in order to remove Flora's outer covering from my sweaters. I noticed that I was rather low on petrol and made a mental note to get some at the first garage that we came to. The only snag was we didn't pass a garage and we swiftly found ourselves in the middle of nowhere with the petrol gauge hard on empty. Mary's route was truly scenic — not a house, not a car, not a person, not even a dog in sight. My anxiety was not aided by Flora flying around the car like a demented wasp and increased even further when we reached a crossroads which miserably failed to have a sign post. With the assurance of the totally ignorant Mrs Thornton told me to go straight over but I was less certain. As luck would have it, we came upon a parked car and a man lounging against the side of it. I decided to stop and ask if we were going in the right direction. I politely wished the man 'Good afternoon' and enquired if we were on the right road for Alford. I might as well have asked him if this was the road to Jupiter judging by the blank stare I received in reply. I tried again with a similar lack of luck. In desperation I got out the map and pointed to Alford. This produced roars or laughter and, "oh you mean Alford". That is what I thought I had said but clearly my pronunciation was not up to scratch. Anyway, happily we were on the right road, Mrs Thornton was pleased

to have been proved right and a few miles further on we came across a garage. Finally, I settled down and began to enjoy myself.

Mrs Thornton never stopped talking and she seemed to know every big house we passed and who lived in it. She was quite determined that we would stop off at one on our way home for a cup of tea. Remembering my predecessors fate I was equally determined that we would have tea in a café in Mablethorpe. The beach at Mablethorpe is long and sandy and a marvellous place for Flora to have a run. However, Mrs Thornton's enthusiasm for an outing didn't actually entail getting out of the car. So Flora and I enjoyed a splendid walk whilst Mrs Thornton sat and snoozed. On our way home we found a delightful café for a late afternoon tea, which neatly forestalled Mrs Thornton's notion of tea in one of the grand mansions we had passed, the owners of which had probably long since departed.

We had both thoroughly enjoyed the day out and I had enjoyed Mrs Thornton's ready wit. If you could manage to ignore the constant repetition, she was very good company. Mrs Thornton's feeling of well-being led to hitting the gin bottle as soon as we arrived home at 6.30 pm. In fact, although she poured lethal drinks, Mrs Thornton didn't actually drink very much. It was just that being a hostess and drinking socially was as much part of her life as breathing and she was the most generous person.

Whilst sipping my drink, a gin and tonic which prudently I had poured, I opened, with considerable trepidation, a letter from Alan which was waiting for me on our return. My heart had sunk when I recognised his handwriting but putting off reading the letter was not going to achieve anything. Actually,

it was a calm and measured letter. Alan had finally accepted that we were unable to work through our problems, that I would not be returning to the matrimonial home and that, therefore, it would be sensible for us to put our separation on a formal footing with a view to an eventual divorce. I couldn't disagree with anything that he had written, and it was actually what I wanted, but nonetheless it was with a great deal of sadness that I realised that our marriage was over. I couldn't just mentally end 23-years in the blink of an eye. Mrs Thornton, who could be incredibly perceptive at times, looked at me kindly and said, "whatever is in that letter is upsetting you but I'm sure that you will work through it. Chin up my dear and pour us both another gin." I really was very fond of Mrs Thornton and she was right, after two hefty gins I definitely began to feel more optimistic and cheerful.

My two weeks with Mrs Thornton had flown by. I spent my last day cooking madly so that there would be some meals in the fridge for when her son arrived to spend a few days with her and then take her to visit her daughter. I would have liked to have met him as Mrs Thornton clearly adored him but he was due to arrive after I had left for my long journey back to Wales. As I left Mrs Thornton showered me with invitations to return and to visit the renowned estate in Scotland, none of which she would remember as soon as my back was turned but it was lovely to be asked. Mrs Thornton was a gem!

# CHAPTER 8

Come back Mr Sinclair, all is forgiven, Mrs Pitt has you beaten into a cocked hat!

I had arrived in Berkshire in high spirits having thoroughly enjoyed my stay with Mrs Thornton followed by a few very productive days in Wales. I had contacted Michael to tell him firstly, that I had decided to enrol on a catering course, the only question being where, and secondly, that I would be in Berkshire for my next assignment and not so very far from him. He had been delighted by the news and said that we must meet up as soon as I had some free time — my heart, rather disturbingly, started to sing. One hour with Mrs Pitt established beyond doubt that I was not up to this type of work on a permanent basis. I lacked the qualities and the stamina required and a new career path was imperative.

I had been greeted by Mrs Anderson, Mrs Pitt's sister, who was an attractive lady and seemed much younger than her sister. She had taken me into a spacious drawing room and I met Mrs Pitt who was perched on the arm of a chair. She was a fairly wild-haired old lady dressed in scruffy clothes — ancient, snagged navy trousers, nylon, white sweater topped by a shapeless and not very clean navy cardigan. Not a vision of great beauty and in complete contrast to her elegant and immaculately dressed sister. Neither did Mrs Pitt look at home in the charming drawing room which was full of antiques, wonderful paintings, priceless china and silver. In fact, the

whole house was the epitome of good taste and wealth.

Mrs Anderson made the obligatory cup of tea but before we could start drinking it an elderly man sidled into the room. My brief communique from the agency described Mrs Pitt as being almost blind. Be that as it may, she spotted this gentleman immediately and very curtly addressed him, "Oh there you are Billings, well you missed her didn't you, much use you are, help her in with her bags". Mrs Pitt took my breath away with her rudeness. I hadn't got a clue who Billings was but I was sure that he didn't deserve to be spoken to in that way, and in case 'her' had a name — Hannah Mills. He grinned sheepishly at me and I meekly followed him out of the room to unlock the car. Once outside he confided in me that the mistress was a difficult one and that most of my predecessors had failed to get on with her. On the face of it I didn't blame them but with good old Grandpa's homily in mind I decided not to prejudge. Apparently poor Billings had been deputed to wait on the corner with the main road in case I missed the turning. He had missed me, because I had arrived a little early, but how on earth he was to have known which was my car, was a mystery. Billings, it transpired, worked in the garden as did another man. Mrs Pitt certainly didn't lack staff. She also had two dailies, one of whom was Mrs Billings and now she had the pleasure of my company to add to her salary bill. Quite why she needed all this help was yet another mystery.

I returned to the drawing room to drink my now cold cup of tea. Mrs Pitt conducted a monologue and neither Mrs Anderson nor I were allowed to open our mouths. Mrs Anderson didn't strike me as a normally cowed sort of person but she was certainly very subdued in her sister's presence. Mrs Pitt had trouble remembering my name so I tentatively

suggested that it might be easier for her to call me Hannah, but oh no, she did not call her staff by their Christian names, such a slack habit! Mrs Thornton would probably have agreed but that would have been the only point on which they were alike.

Tea finished Mrs Anderson guided Mrs Pitt into her wheelchair and then left looking very relieved. Mrs Pitt demanded a double brandy and soda and commanded me to wheel her into her bedroom, which was on the ground floor — it was 4.30 pm! As I left her clasping her mammoth drink to her equally mammoth bosom I asked if I could use the telephone to let the agency know that I had arrived safely. I didn't intend to use my newly acquired and expensive mobile phone for business purposes. Mrs Pitt graciously gave me permission to use the telephone on her bedside table. When I had finished, she took the phone to speak to the agency herself and I left the room. It wasn't a question of intentional eavesdropping, I should think the passers-by in the street could have heard Mrs Pitt's conversation with the agency, and it was very illuminating. In extremely strident terms she expressed the hope that I would stay for the full three weeks. She really couldn't understand why the previous helpers had been unhappy with her and had never stayed the course, she was so undemanding! Grandpa notwithstanding, I had a nasty feeling that this time first impressions were going to stick. My first impression was that Mrs Pitt was thoroughly unpleasant and a crashing snob into the bargain.

Mrs Pitt was an infirm widow of 85 with failing eyesight. Following a fall some months ago she had become nervous about getting around and had resorted to a wheelchair, hence the need for a helper. The usual thumbnail sketch from the agency informed me that Mrs Pitt required a little help with .

dressing and in the bathroom and that the wheelchair was only used outside. This sketch proved to be the understatement of the year. I swiftly discovered that Mrs Pitt had to be assisted with everything. She was a crafty old woman. She could still accomplish quite a lot for herself but had abandoned any attempt to do so. She quite obviously intended to get her money's worth out of the hired help. She had to be helped in and out of her wheelchair and, although she was perfectly capable of wheeling it herself, always demanded that I wheel her. Despite her insistence that I should be called by my surname she couldn't be bothered to remember it and tended to just yell "Mrs," when she needed me. This irritated me so much that I took to ignoring her summons until she addressed me properly. It wasn't a question of a failing memory, just sheer laziness and a lack of courtesy.

Mrs Pitt was not a tall woman but considerably overweight and it took me all my strength to transfer her from her wheelchair to her armchair or bed and getting her into the shower required a superhuman effort. She had designed an ingenious Heath Robinson set up for the shower which had been installed in the cloakroom. A non-slip mat was placed on the floor of the shower and an old kitchen chair was place on the mat so Mrs Pitt could sit whilst she showered. It worked brilliantly (if only Mrs Thornton had possessed a shower, we could have adopted the idea) but the transition from wheelchair to kitchen chair was exceptionally tricky. Mrs Pitt didn't believe in cooperating and she was like a deadweight. I would be lucky if my back survived the next three weeks let alone anything else, most notably my temper. Mrs Pitt's ablutions took a very long time. Having showered she would sit there and demand first one sort of cream, followed by

talcum powder, followed by another sort of cream, one oil for her face and finally I had to put a different oil on her feet (she couldn't do that herself and she probably had illusions of being celestial). It never occurred to her to utter a please or a thank you and her tone was unpleasantly abrupt, sometimes almost a snarl. Fortunately, I swiftly learnt in what order Mrs Pitt applied this myriad of aids to beauty and comfort because the first morning she was completely exasperated with my inability to know, intuitively, what she required. Why she bothered with all this paraphernalia defeated me because the tiresome ritual did nothing to improve either her looks or her temperament, but perhaps it helped keep sores away.

Mrs Pitt was also completely paranoid about burglars. Every night I had to go round the house and double lock the front door, double lock the back door, lock the inner door, draw all the curtains and bolt the doors to the drawing room, dining room, kitchen, cloakroom and inner hall. Then I had to set the burglar alarm and deliver the keys into Mrs Pitt's safe keeping for the night. In the morning I had to go through the whole performance in reverse. All the windows were locked and double glazed. The house was kept so hot that I knew I would never sleep unless I had a window open. However, it was with considerable reluctance that I was allowed a key and thus able to let a breath of fresh air into my bedroom.

Even then sleep was not a luxury I was able to indulge in except in fits and starts. Mrs Pitt didn't sleep well herself, despite taking vast quantities of tranquillizers, sleeping pills and any other medication she could lay her hands on, so she kept the radio playing all night, not quietly but at full volume. Additionally, the hall light had to remain lit during the supposed hours of repose, which was quite unnecessary

because Mrs Pitt never left her room at night and if caught short, she used a commode. My bedroom door was made of diffused glass and thus the light from the hall downstairs shone in. Going to bed was somewhat similar to attempting slumber in an all-night disco, which was not very conducive to maintaining a serene and composed manner during the daytime. Lack of sleep makes me very irritable and so it became a matter of honour not to give Mrs Pitt the satisfaction of making me lose my temper. Three weeks of this seemed like an eternity.

The saving grace of the situation were Mrs Pitt's two dailies, Mrs Cave and Mrs Billings. Mrs Cave was very similar to Mr Sinclair's Maggie and came on Monday, Tuesday and Friday. Mrs Billings, wife of Billings, came on Wednesday and Thursday and was superb at providing tea and sympathy for the poor helper. She invited me, and all my predecessors, to tea in the afternoon as a respite and as far as I could gather, we had all accepted with alacrity. It soon became apparent that, delightful as each daily was, there was a considerable rivalry between the priceless pair and they never met if they could help it. Nonetheless they both agreed that Mrs Pitt was an extremely difficult employer, but Mrs Pitt knew how to retain her staff, she paid them extremely well.

My first morning was Mrs Cave's day on duty. I knew that she arrived at 8.00 am and let herself in with her own keys. I realised, therefore, that it was imperative to have the burglar alarm switched off before she arrived, otherwise we would have bells ringing, lights flashing and me with not a clue how to stop them. Mrs Pitt had ordered tea in bed at 7.50 am which I thought should give me ample time to retrieve the keys and turn off the alarm. I had reckoned without Mrs Cave arriving

early. As I was making for the end of the inner hall, where the alarm was situated, I heard a key rattle in the back door. In fact, it was Mrs Pitt's paranoia that saved the day. Mrs Cave had two locks to tackle before she could open the door and that gave me sufficient time to dash and switch the alarm off. I think Mrs Cave was more than a bit surprised to find me gasping as though I had just run a 100-metre sprint. She was like a mother hen, clucking around making soothing noises, and she insisted on making me a cup of coffee in the kitchen to calm me down.

It was only later that I realised that the rivalry between the two dailies extended to outdoing each other in their care of the current helper. That first morning I thought it slightly odd that Mrs Cave insisted on doing the shopping list. I wasn't allowed to do a thing and I was made to sit in the kitchen drinking coffee whilst she bustled around deciding what was needed. I found it rather disconcerting as I was the one who was going to be doing the cooking. In the end I decided to assert my authority marginally and I gently told Mrs Cave that I would discuss with Mrs Pitt what she wanted to eat. Mrs Cave smiled sweetly back and said, "what a good idea, you do that dear," and determinedly continued to write her list. Mrs Pitt, when consulted, maintained that she ate nothing but pap and gruel. It sounded deathly boring and I had never made anything that remotely resembled pap or gruel in my life. Further subtle questioning, however, elicited the fact that soup and smoked salmon sandwiches usually constituted lunch with perhaps an orange or cheese and biscuits. Supper was either porridge or egg custard. Not a very inspiring diet and certainly not one which would tax my cooking abilities to any great degree. When I returned to the kitchen Mrs Cave handed me, with a

wry smile, her neatly written list which contained everything I would require for Mrs Pitt's dietary needs. Mrs Pitt seemed to acquire most of her calories through alcohol. She had at least two large gins and sodas before lunch and two large brandies and sodas before supper. Mrs Pitt had no intention of running out of her favourite beverages either. The store cupboard already had a plentiful supply of both, but on my first morning Mrs Pitt rang Augustus Barnett to request them to deliver yet more. Despite the fact that the house was awash with booze, if we ever had a flood here it would be alcoholic one, I was never invited to join her in a gin and tonic or even a gin and soda!

The days dragged by enlightened only by the thought of my first day off and lunch with Michael. We had agreed to meet in the same wine bar in Guildford where we previously had had lunch. Finally, my day off dawned and I jumped out of bed with enthusiasm, gone were the leaden feet of yesterday. I don't know if Mrs Pitt did it on purpose (although I suspect that she did) but she decided that today she would have her hair washed. This entailed my practically having to get into the shower with her and after all that steam Mrs Pitt had clean hair but my freshly washed hair hung limp and straggly and my carefully applied makeup was in tatters. The news was currently full of appalling tales of assaults, rapes and murders. After the hair washing episode there was a grave danger that the murder of an elderly widow in Berkshire might well be added to the ever-growing list of terrible crimes.

I repaired the damage to both hair and make-up as best I could and then left with a squeal of tyres and the air thick with invective. Fortunately, my journey was trouble free and I made it to the wine bar only a few minutes late. Michael rose on seeing me, with his face lit up by his wonderful infectious grin,

and my heart started the singing business again. Once again, we ordered drinks and something to eat and it was just so good to be in a 'normal' setting for a change. I told Michael all about Mrs Thornton and now Mrs Pitt the words fairly tumbling out of me. He roared with laughter over my trials and tribulations with Mrs Pitt and completely agreed with me that a new career was imperative. We discussed further the idea of a catering course. I was becoming more and more enamoured with the idea and I really enjoyed cooking. The next issue, therefore, had to be where to do such a course. The moment had come to tell Michael that Alan had finally accepted that I wasn't going to return to him, that our marriage had irretrievably broken down and that a divorce, in the fullness of time, was inevitable. Given this position I could look to anywhere to retrain and I had been giving the matter much thought. Staying in the Liverpool area held no attractions for me and Wales, whilst lovely in the summer, was very remote in the winter and with no nearby colleges of further education. Both Nick and Simon appeared to have their sights firmly set on the bright lights of London for their careers, so to be in the south of England would make sense. I had lived my entire childhood in Surrey and had immediately felt at home when staying with the Chadwicks and Mr Sinclair — I was so familiar with the countryside, the towns and villages. So my thoughts were turning to Guildford College and the full-time catering courses on offer there. My research had shown me that the entry requirement for the Food, Beverage & Professional Cookery Level 2 Diploma was 4 GCSEs. GCSEs were way before my time but I did have 10 'O' levels so, hopefully, I was eligible. Michael's face lit up when I tentatively suggested this idea and he announced it perfect. He was also impressed by the quantity

of my exam results. He hadn't remembered me as being a girly swot which was not surprising. My parents hadn't encouraged me to do 'A' levels and I had only just turned 18 when we first met all those years ago. At that time having fun was my priority not academic qualifications. However, even with the necessary entry requirement there was still the hurdle of being accepted on the course and finding somewhere to live, but September was a long way off. Feeling that much had been accomplished we then sat back, enjoyed our lunch and continued to fill each other in with what had been happening in the last 26 years.

I returned to Mrs Pitt feeling very uplifted, and with my head buzzing with ideas and plans, to find Mrs Anderson sitting with her sister. It was about 5.00 pm and Mrs Pitt was clasping her mandatory brandy and soda in a vice like grip. Mrs Anderson didn't have a drink, maybe she had been offered one but had refused feeling that it was a little early in the day for hard alcohol. However, when Mrs Pitt commanded me to refresh her tumbler, she didn't press Mrs Anderson to join her. Mrs Anderson chatted to me quite pleasantly, she was clearly dying to know where I had been so smartly dressed, but I had no intention of letting Mrs Pitt know anything about my life outside her four walls. I need not have worried that Mrs Pitt might be even remotely interested and she soon resumed her customary self-centred monologue and, after standing for fifteen minutes as naturally I was not asked to sit down, I felt extremely tired. Fortunately, Mrs Anderson decided to leave before I actually dropped with fatigue and I was then able to give Mrs Pitt her porridge for supper and get her ready for bed.

Having settled my charge for the night I first wrote a letter to Guildford College applying to enrol on the Food, Beverage

& Professional Cookery Level 2 Diploma and then I took my mobile telephone into the drawing and telephoned Penny to update her on my lunch with Michael and my plans for the future. Liverpool seemed such a long way from Berkshire but distance is of no matter when you can chat on the telephone. Soon we were in gales of laughter and I should have realised that the noise would disturb Mrs Pitt, who had very acute hearing and a very powerful pair of lungs. Sure enough, before long Mrs Pitt bellowed, "who is that on the telephone?"

I went and having placatingly explained that I was calling a friend and that this call was on my mobile telephone and not on the house telephone, I returned to the drawing room and my call. After a while I thought I heard a noise in the hall and knowing Mrs Pitt's fear of burglars, I told Penny to hold the line whilst I went to investigate. In the hall, to my amazement, was Mrs Pitt obviously eavesdropping. This was the woman who persistently maintained that she was immobile, and had to be wheeled everywhere, standing on her own two feet having walked from her bedroom. I was so angry, but I didn't dare say anything because if I had there would have been explosions all round. I just turned on my heel, returned to the drawing room, shut the door and resumed my call with Penny. Presumably, Mrs Pitt made her own way safely back to bed because that is where I found her the next morning.

That next morning Mrs Pitt declared an armed truce, not in so many words and she certainly didn't refer to her nocturnal escapade, but she did make an effort to be pleasant and I even received the odd please and thank you. Despite the temptation to walk out, I had committed myself for the next ten days, I needed the money but above all I didn't like to admit that I had been defeated by a little old lady. I began to

think that the episode had, in fact, saved the whole situation and we seemed to get along much better.

When it came to doing the shopping for the weekend, I tried to persuade Mrs Pitt that if I bought a chicken, I could roast it for lunch on Saturday and then casserole the remains for lunch on Sunday, it would make a pleasant change to her normal diet. Amazingly she agreed and further went on to suggest that we could have baked apples for pudding. Not only that she decided that she would like to eat this feast in the dining room and graciously invited me to join her — she normally ate her pap and gruel on a trolley in her bedroom in blissful solitude. We were definitely into a ceasefire situation and, when Mrs Pitt commanded me to find a decent bottle of white wine in the store cupboard to go with lunch, I felt that peace negotiations stood a fair chance of succeeding. Certainly, the weekend passed peacefully enough. I had read the headlines from the *Daily Mail* to Mrs Pitt and she had enjoyed her lunches. The sun had shone and she had sat quietly in the porch gaining some fresh air. We had even managed some desultory conversation. I learnt that Mrs Pitt had been one of five children but that she only had her sister, Mrs Anderson, still alive. She had married late in life to an extremely wealthy man but they never had any children. She had clearly been used to a very pampered lifestyle and just as clearly was incapable of thinking much beyond herself and how events affected her. I tried to be charitable and put her self-centredness down to exasperation with her present infirmity, pain and inability to do things for herself but she made that a difficult task. Every so often I would catch her being quite nimble and capable and she had certainly been nimble enough when she had leapt out of bed to do her

eavesdropping act.

Monday morning, however, brought our truce to a juddering halt. Monday brought the return of Mrs Cave and the return of Mrs Pitt's desire for the value for money. If she was paying two people to help, then there was to be no slacking. Having completed her shower Mrs Pitt detailed me to clean the shower cum cloak room which I did very thoroughly but unwillingly, cleaning didn't actually come within my remit. Having finished Mrs Cave then beetled in, with rubber gloves on, ready to start cleaning. I explained that I had already done it. Mrs Cave smiled sweetly, ignored me and got scrubbing. I walked out of the room in bewilderment to be greeted by the dulcet tones of Mrs Pitt who demanded to know if I had done the job properly and to remember that it wasn't my day off. We were definitely back to square one.

However, I saw a very different side to Mrs Pitt's character when the doctor came to call. I had been ordered to summon him on a house visit because he hadn't been recently. I could only presume that Mrs Pitt was a private patient because I felt sure that the National Health Service had better ways to spend its money than pandering to the whim of spoilt old ladies. When the doctor arrived, Mrs Pitt was charm personified and I was left doing an excellent impression of a goldfish with my mouth wide open in amazement. She chatted and smiled and laughingly said that the next time the doctor called he should bring a gun with him instead of his prescription pad. For all the world she appeared to be a wonderful old lady putting a brave face on her ill health and incapacitation. The doctor clearly thought she was marvellous but the minute I had shut the front door on him the far from incapacitated lungs were yelling "Mrs". The whole situation

was straight out of a Victorian novel which made me feel better. Instead of being permanently on the verge of tears I felt like laughing and promptly did, which startled Mrs Pitt. She was unaccustomed to hearing her browbeaten staff in high spirits.

Every afternoon Mrs Pitt graciously gave me (although actually that was my entitlement) two hours off from 2—4 pm whilst she snoozed in her armchair. I took to going out for every second of those two hours. One day, when it was pouring with rain, I had decided to stay in and read my book which was a big mistake. Knowing that I was in the house Mrs Pitt kept demanding my assistance to go to the bathroom and I never even finished a chapter. However, what to do with these two hours was a poser. Michael was working and if I drove round the countryside, which I knew reasonably well anyway, all I would be doing was spending a fortune in petrol. Then I hit on the bright idea of going to visit Doris and finding out if her future had been settled. She lived sufficiently near for me to be able to get there, have a cup of tea and be back within the stated two hours. On the dot of 2.00 pm I waved goodbye to my current charge and disappeared. Doris was delighted to see me, not that for a moment did I flatter myself that she remembered who I was, she just enjoyed visitors and had a naturally welcoming temperament. What a difference — I would have willingly exchanged the wealth, comfort and comparative freedom of Mrs Pitt's sumptuous home for the cold, decrepitude and constant vigilance required in Doris's home. She looked well, alert and chatty. Her current helper was a bouncy, cheerful soul and Doris was clearly happy in her company. It was good to realise that her improved state had been maintained and that she had not regressed into the

confused, sad, old lady that I had originally met. What was even better, I learnt that her nephew had organised a place for her in the local Methodist's care home and that she would be moving there shortly. I was so glad that I had come, seeing Doris and hearing her news made the job seem definitely worthwhile. I went back to my demanding tyrant in a much happier frame of mind.

The style in which Mrs Pitt lived was, without question, light years removed from Doris's existence on an old age pension and Ted's hard-earned savings. I discovered that every week the hairdresser came to do Mrs Pitt's hair (so she had made me wash her hair on purpose) and every week a manicurist appeared on the doorstep to do her nails. Her resulting immaculate nails looked so incongruous with her badly groomed appearance and the weekly visit of the hairdresser only ever created a transitory improvement. Despite all this activity Mrs Pitt still continually complained of boredom and that she never saw the helpers who were supposed to be looking after her. On my second day she asked me what I did in my room. Without bothering to allow me to reply she said sourly, "I expect you are making bombs!"

Oh, if only I was that proficient. I would then be able to put one under her bed and thus end both her misery and mine! Apart from tending to her constant needs, to spend any other time with her was difficult. As soon as I had delivered her tea or coffee, gin or brandy I was peremptorily dismissed. In a last-ditch effort to do my job properly, as I saw it, I took to buying a daily paper and reading her the main articles. The first time, which had been during our cease-fire over the weekend, had been quite successful. The second time she stopped me after five minutes, bored as usual, and the third

time she never even let me get started since she had already heard the news ten times over on the radio. I gave up.

Fortunately for my sanity I received a very prompt reply from Guildford College who wished to interview me with a view to enrolling me on my preferred catering course. I was really heartened and fortuitously an interview was arranged for the day that my allotted span with Mrs Pitt came to an end. To drive all the way from Wales to Guildford for an interview would have been quite arduous. Thus, during my last few days with Mrs Pitt her troublesome personality became merely peripheral to my thought processes — I had my interview to contemplate. The agency hadn't given me an interview, which really was quite remiss of them considering the vulnerability of some of the people the helpers have to look after, the agency had simply taken up my references. My last interview had been many years ago and was when the head of the mafia decided that I needed some occupation to keep me out of mischief (I wasn't permitted to work) and had put my name forward as a prospective magistrate.

It had seemed like a good idea at the time but my subsequent interview closely resembled the Spanish Inquisition. On arriving at the Magistrates Courts, I had been met by an extremely pleasant court clerk who took me to the Magistrates retiring room, a very imposing place. I had sat nervously, with knees knocking, for what seemed like an eternity until I was invited to enter the inner sanctum. Keen to make a good impression I had put a smile on my face and walked towards the lady and gentleman standing behind a table with my arm outstretched ready to shake hands. I was considerably taken aback to be told that the Advisory Committee was a secret one and that they were unable to

introduce themselves. It all sounded a bit cloak and dagger to me and I just felt incredibly stupid standing there with my hand waving in the breeze. Even if I was forbidden from knowing their identities, secrecy surely need not have prevented them from shaking hands. I would have thought common courtesy demanded it. Not a good start!

The well-upholstered, imposing lady with the splendidly blue-rinsed hair, a delicate shade of forget-me-not (and I certainly would never forget her) opened the interview. Before her she had my painstakingly completed application form which she glanced through quickly and then announced that they wished to confirm that everything I had written there was correct. She started at the top and asked if I was Hannah Anna Mills. She struck me as a stickler for accuracy and I am not Anna, I am Anne, so I told her so. Unfortunately, the lady may have been imposing but she seemed unable to grasp the difference between the two versions of the same name. Perhaps she thought that 'Hannah Anna' had a good rhythmic ring to it. After labouring the point for some time, I began to despair and really did it matter, it was only my second name when all was said and done. Eventually we progressed to different topics but by that time I had been reduced to jelly and could only summon up monosyllabic replies (no wonder I had felt such sympathy for Mrs Smith after her interview with Mr Sinclair). The formidable lady was clearly in charge but the gentleman was permitted to ask three questions and it was the same each time with minor variations:

Question 1: "You have put on your application form that you are a Conservative is that correct?" Answer: "Yes."

Question 2: "It is important that we keep the bench properly balanced and therefore it is essential that we know

your political persuasion. Is it accurate to class you as a Conservative?" Answer: "Yes."

Question 3: "Are you absolutely certain that you are a Conservative?" Answer: "Yes."

I couldn't understand this repetition of the same question. Surely politics shouldn't play a part in the work of a magistrate and, although I could appreciate the need for an evenly balanced bench, surely this type of third-degree interrogation was unnecessary. Perhaps it was all part of a devious plot to see if I was easily rattled. The interview lurched from bad to worse and the formidable lady concluded with what was evidently her favourite question:

"Mrs Mills do you have any personal prejudices that might interfere with your ability to make impartial decisions? For instance, I do not like red hair so if someone comes into Court with that coloured hair I have to mentally blank it from my mind."

I could hardly say that I lacked any prejudices so I wracked my currently non-existent brain and came with a reply which was perfectly honest:

"I don't like rude people. I think rudeness is unnecessary."

To which came the very sharp retort: "Oh like people who call you Anna when you are just Anne"

End of interview! I went home in tears feeling completely decimated. Needless to say I was not appointed as a magistrate. Now I just hoped that my interview with Guildford College would have a happier outcome. It did, and I was to start my chosen course in September. I was not sure whether I would be able to cope with all the studying and practical work but I felt full of enthusiasm. If nothing else, the last few months

had taught me how to adapt and learn, abilities which had, hitherto, not been very apparent."

I left Mrs Pitt with a feeling of immense relief. I hadn't enjoyed my time with her and despite eventually reaching a state of cautious neutrality I felt a distinct failure. At least with Mr Sinclair I had left with a sense of achievement. After my interview I returned to Wales in a mood of considerable optimism. There was much still to achieve — separation, divorce, financial settlement, telling Nick and Simon with all the emotion and sadness that those talks would entail, moving, finding a new home, the list seemed endless. Nonetheless the future now looked much brighter and when I woke each morning I actually wanted to get out of bed.

# EPILOGUE

It is now Christmas 2020. We have been through a second lockdown but the pandemic continues. A four-tier system, applied regionally, has been introduced to try and control the spread of the disease. However, with the emergence of a rampant mutant strain of the virus, a third national lockdown seems almost inevitable.

Morale is not high. There has been great suffering and hardship, in comparison with which my past struggles pale into insignificance. Nonetheless, everyone has been amazingly resilient with their sense of humour well intact, if the constant stream of hilarious and topical jokes on social media is anything to judge by. The world is still a troubled and rather scary place to live in, but there is light at the end of the tunnel. The indomitable scientists have worked around the clock, vaccines have been developed, tried and tested and a programme of vaccination has already commenced. Hopefully this programme will slowly enable life to regain some semblance of normality.

The world will probably never be the same again. It will take a long time for the economy to recover and for fractured lives and livelihoods to rebuild, but in doing so, with luck, it may just develop to become a better world. A bit like the phoenix rising out of the ashes!

I am sitting on the sofa in my comfortable home and Michael comes in holding two glasses of wine. With his still

infectious grin and in his still wonderfully sexy voice he says, "Remember the cartoon that kept us all amused during the first lockdown — if you keep a glass of wine in each hand you can't touch your face?" My wide smile in response says it all.

# About the Author

Mary McLaurin was born in Cambridge and has since lived in various parts of the UK. She has two sons and leads a busy life.